GARRET'S
GAME
a Boys & Toys novella

by

Daryl Banner

Author of

Bromosexual

Hard For My Boss

Football Sundae

&

The Brazen Boys Series

Garret's Game
A Boys & Toys Novella

Cover Photography & Model
Nathan Hainline

Cover & Interior Design
Daryl Banner

The Boys & Toys Series

✳

✳

GARRET'S GAME
CHAPTER LIST

GARRET'S
GAME
a Boys & Toys novella

[1]

Garret's phone alarm plays Chopin's Nocturne in E-flat major, opus 9 number 2. It's been playing for a minute already, but Garret hasn't gotten out of bed. He stares at a shadow on his ceiling and listens to each carefully stroked note of music. It is easy to imagine his boss sitting at a piano playing this very piece, his broad, strong back facing him. Garret's heart surges longingly at the thought.

GARRET

Everything is different now.

My boss and I haven't spoken a word about the exchange we had in his office two weeks ago.

The day I outed myself as a fetishist, and he—indirectly, at least—outed himself, too.

Mr. Kevin Kingston is one handsome enigma to me. A keen, authoritative, handsome enigma.

Just the sound of his voice makes me stiffen up with excitement. It's not the kind of excitement that only lives in the mind; it's the kind that turns my stomach over in a thrilling way, like a roller coaster, unsettling me with an unspoken promise of all my fantasies being fulfilled, that takes prisoner my whole body and doesn't dare let me go.

Mr. Kevin Kingston isn't a gorgeous man. If it wasn't for my kinky mind creating a whole world centered around him, you might even find Kevin's face to be too plain. Forgettable, even.

But that's because you, as a casual observer of the deceivingly-average man that is my boss, are being robbed of the most important key element of a person that makes them sexy to a guy like me:

Context.

You'll walk past him on account of a plain face and not overly-musclebound body—and not know how *owned* that man could make you feel with just a single carefully-worded question directed right at you.

You won't bother to look twice at a guy like him—and utterly miss the fact that if you worked under him every day for almost two years, you would have a whole new dark appreciation for calling your superiors "sir"—like I do.

You might not swipe right on him, but that's because you haven't heard the near-condescending yet totally-attentive voice he'll use when he calls you into his office and, in a completely calm yet firm voice, asks for a report on your progress.

And you stand there before him, squirming inside, wanting to piss your pants, and at the same time desperately hoping to please him.

You always want to please him.

You don't even know why anymore.

Is this what true love is? Or is it some fucked-up, unhealthy dynamic that some prudish person would look down on me for, claiming I'm a victim of psychological abuse?

If craving to be beneath him is so unhealthy, then why does it make me feel so good?

Even if I get nothing in return but unending sexual frustration and deeper longing?

I rise from my bed in a huff and allow the alarm to continue playing Chopin's Nocturne in E-flat while I go to the bathroom to take my long morning leak, wash my weary face, and jump in the shower.

I'm one of those shower-twice-a-day guys.

Cleanliness is next to godliness, they say.

And my god is Kevin Kingston.

While still in just my tight white cotton Calvin Klein boxer-briefs, I walk over to the tiny window of my second-story corner apartment overlooking the intersection to get a glimpse of the world today. Everything looks gray and early-morningish.

I move away from the window and bump into my tiny round dining room table.

My eyes land on a small box.

Oh. I forgot about that.

With my lips puckered up in thought, I pick up the box and turn it over, reading the back of it for the twentieth time since receiving it yesterday. "*Saw this and thought you might like a little self-punishing fun for a change. Sincerely, Jeremy.*"

I smirk.

What an odd message to sign "sincerely" at the bottom of.

I didn't have the energy (or a horny-enough frame of mind) to open the box last night, so I left it here. Also, Jeremy is my former booty call for anything fetish, and I felt strange accepting a gift from him. We had a falling out (if it can be called that) and really don't hook up or get off together anymore. We do, however, still keep in touch.

But he's never sent me a little box before.

What is it? A bottle of cherry-flavored lube? (Not that my dick tastes anything when I jerk off.)

A shock collar for my balls? (Shocking.)

A Captain America butt plug?

Stubborn thoughts of my boss linger in every part of my mind. Ever since Revelation Day, as I like to call it, I spend twice as long in the closet laboring over which tie to wear each morning. Will red set a better impression on Mr. Kingston, or will I look sharper in all black? Which color best says "please own me in every way, sir"? Which pattern screams "I want to be a permanent member of your team, as long as you are the coach-captain-leader-master, and are always fiercely critical with me."

I think that's the reason I open the box today.

With a popping open of each side, I slide out a small vinyl pouch labeled: *COCK-LOCK 3000.*

Well, those words are quite an introduction.

This might be messed up, but for a moment, I pretend it isn't Jeremy who's sent the gift. For the sake of building up a fantasy, I tell myself that it's Mr. Kevin Kingston who sent me this package.

You're going to put this on, Kevin demands. *No matter what it is. No matter what it'll do to you. No matter the consequence, you will wear it.*

"Yes, sir," I say out loud.

Then I open the vinyl pouch and peer inside.

My lips part. My eyes widen.

"Oh, f-fuck," I hear myself breathe out.

You will wear it, Kevin demands.

Slowly, I pull the toy out of the pouch. I stare at the small metal cage where a cock is supposed to go. I turn it over and look at the ring where a pair of balls are supposed to go through. Along its base, a tiny hole lives where a tiny padlock can hang, ready to be clicked shut, locking the cage in place with strict, firm pressure.

It's an efficient toy. An evil, efficient toy.

"I'm ... not really gonna put this on my dick, am I?" I ask out loud.

Yes, you are, answers Kevin. I imagine him wiggling the metal chastity cage in front of me. *It's going to be really fun for me to own your dick for a couple of days. Or a week. Or maybe the rest of the month. However long you can take it.*

"Those are ... deadly words," I mutter, tension in my voice. "You know I ... never quite learned how to say enough is enough."

I know, states Kevin coolly. *Always asking for more torment. More and more and more.*

The way he says those words in my mind, so matter-of-fact, so devoid of emotion, so robotic, I find it unsettlingly sexy. Like it's a fact.

So? Imaginary Kevin nods at my very-real and very-present bulge in my tight, white Calvin Klein boxer-briefs. *You ready to cram your pent-up cock into this contraption? Once I click that cage shut with this padlock, it's a sentence. The key belongs to me, and you are mine until I let you out.*

I gulp.

It's a loud, certain, audible gulp.

My heart races with excitement as my eyes drop once again to this toy in my palm—this evil, cruel, cock-punishing toy. I imagine my junk as it is crammed into this cage whether I like it or not, fixed firmly against my body, denying me even the pleasure of a full erection. What an evil thing to do to another man, especially when he's already so damned horny and hasn't had the time or energy to jerk off for the past three days.

It's perfect.

"Yes, sir," I answer Kevin. "I'm ready, sir."

Then I tug my underwear halfway down my thighs, exposing my throbbing boner.

It's the last full boner I'll have for a while.

I watch it with sinking dread as I wait with forced patience for my overly excited, tragically unknowing dick to soften.

It takes a while.

When it's soft, I slip my balls through the base ring, fitting it against my body like a cock ring, except this one is ready to wear a cruelly curved metal hat. I carefully pull the metal cock cage out of the vinyl pouch and, after taking a quick steeling breath, slip my cock inside it. It's cold. Then I slip the tiny padlock through the holes and click it shut, fastening the cage to the base ring.

I stare down at my junk, now trapped in a mostly discreet, slim metal contraption. It's small and compact enough that I doubt it'll show through any clothes I wear. No one will know it's there but me—*and imaginary Kevin*. It even has an opening at the end of the cage to allow for calls of nature.

How thoughtful.

I pull my underwear up over it. As predicted, the cage barely makes a bulge. *I think I'm gonna like this*, I tell myself, feeling horny and cautiously excited. I move to the closet, testing how it feels when I walk. Except for the tiniest bit of noticeable weight, I hardly know it's there.

As I pick out my tie with an added pinch of confidence, I realize maybe this is exactly what I needed: to bring my *fun* into the workplace where Mr. Kevin Kingston himself is.

Maybe I'll see this as a kind of ... *game.*

A game where I win every time.

Every day.

Every shift.

My little metal secret.

I pick out a crisp white shirt to wear, along with a pair of fitted and particularly butt-hugging black skinny-leg dress pants. After sliding on a black belt, I pull out a slim green tie and start to meticulously tie a double Windsor in front of the mirror, smirking at myself with dark amusement.

I've never felt more ready to strut into that office than I do today.

WADE

I stir awake at the sound of metal clattering in my kitchen.

I sit up, alarmed.

Then, as if the memory slowly pours over me like a thick and viscous syrup, I remember falling asleep next to someone in my apartment last night.

My fingers glide across the other side of my bed, now just a crumpled mess of bed sheets and a pillow with a head-sized indent still pressed into it.

Caysen's head, to be exact.

My best friend.

Or whatever he is now.

I check the time (it's approximately way-too-fucking-early o'clock), then slip into the bathroom to relieve myself. *Why is peeing in the morning the sweetest relief, sweeter even than sex?* Afterwards, I pull on a pair of long, gray shiny gym shorts sans underwear, then come down the hall to the kitchen.

Caysen—totally naked except for an apron—is busy at the counter making us breakfast. I smell eggs mostly, but there are definitely a few other things going on at that counter I can't quite make out from over here.

Not that I'm paying attention to any of it. I'm staring down at my best friend's tight, plump, pert muscled ass, cinched right above by the tie of the apron he's wearing. My eyes drag up his V-shaped muscled backside, all his rippling back muscles, and that sexy valley that runs up the middle, right up between his two powerful shoulder blades and the thick muscles that give them a fuller shape. His slanting, corded traps smoothly crawl up the base of his neck, flexing a bit as Caysen's head bobs to some song in his head while he cooks breakfast, chipper and energetic.

He's always been like this, ever since our days of being roommates in college. An early-riser, he was out of bed first damned thing and jogging laps around campus before his first class. It's admirable, really, his dedication to the great and glorious temple of his work-of-art body.

Caysen peers over his shoulder, sensing me. His warm eyes meet mine. A smile spreads over his face. "Good morning, buddy." His gaze skips down to my bare chest. I watch him suck on his tongue a second before he adds, "You're looking rather refreshed ... especially after last night."

Last night was certainly something else.

I let out one breathless chuckle, then return a nod. "I feel …" I smile back too. "… refreshed."

He winks at me, then nods at the table. "Take a seat. Breakfast is almost ready."

"Smells delicious."

"It is. And healthy," he adds. "I went down to the corner and got some bacon."

I quirk an eyebrow. "Bacon is healthy?"

Caysen shoots me a look. "It's turkey. And fat-free. Have we met?" He snorts and returns his full attention to the counter, granting me another show of his tight buns.

I sit down at the tiny table by the window. He even set the table for breakfast. I stare at my plate, fork, napkin, and a glass of orange juice. I pick it up to take a sip and, to my surprise, find it cold, as if freshly poured.

"Heard you waking up," Caysen throws over his shoulder. "I know you like your orange juice first thing. You get cranky without it."

I set my glass down. "You know me so well."

He smirks superiorly, then snatches the spatula and starts scraping at the pan of eggs.

I watch him, smiling.

Boyfriend.

I gently gnaw on my bottom lip, trying to hear that word in my head without panicking somehow.

Boyfriend.

Caysen Ryan. Boyfriend.

I bring a finger to my mouth, mulling it over.

Caysen Ryan …

I take another sip of my orange juice, glance at the window for a second's reprieve from Caysen's ass, then look right back at his buns, heart racing.

Best friend. Boyfriend.

Best friend. Boyfriend.

The words all sound so strange now. Both of them. Even Caysen's name rhymes with the weird and weirder terms. *Boyfriend Caysen. Best friend Caysen. Caysen. Boyfriend. Best friend. Caysen.*

I take another sip. My fingers are particularly twitchy. There's a tick starting in my right eyelid.

Why are those ideas so difficult to marry? *Best friend, boyfriend. Best friend, boyfriend.*

Marry.

Fuck, another word.

Best friend. Boyfriend. Caysen. Marry.

I clench shut my eyes, then take a full gulp of my juice. Some goes down the wrong way and I start coughing and sputtering, setting my glass down at once, eyes clenched shut as I cough away.

There's hands on my arm and back.

I flinch and flap my eyes open.

Caysen's right there. "You okay?"

"Wrong pipe," I answer, rasping and wincing.

"Ah, okay." He smirks, gives my back a loving little rub, then nods at my glass. "Better slow down there before you drink the whole thing. Breakfast's coming up, and we need you well-fed before your rehearsal." Caysen goes back to the stove, then asks, "When does your show open again?"

I answer to his broad backside. "Next week."

"Next week," he repeats thoughtfully.

My watery eyes drop once more to his ass. I stare at those two tight ass cheeks like they're made of solid gold. My napkin is suddenly caught between my hands like a prisoner. While slowly wringing it, I keep trying on those innocent words in the changing room of my brain like stiff, unfamiliar jackets fresh off the rack.

Best friend ...

Caysen ...

Boyfriend ...

DEAN

"So what do you think of my plan?"

Sam slurps on his coffee by the window, then studies me with a twinkle in his eye. "Babe, I think it sounds perfect."

"It's been a long time since you've gone out with us," I point out. "It'll be like a double date. Except we can't call it that."

"Definitely not," Sam agrees knowingly.

"But it *is* a double date."

"Definitely. Is Garret—?"

"Nope. He's *so* not into the idea. I think he and Jeremy might be getting back together ... or maybe I misread that text he sent me last night about a 'belated birthday present' he got. I think he's in one of his *reclusive phases*. He tells me nothing."

Sam shrugs, then eyes me over his mug. "You know, they're lucky to have you as their friend."

I frown. "Why do you say that?"

Sam sets his mug down, rises from his chair, and comes around to the back of mine. He puts his strong hands on my shoulders, and when he starts to massage, I melt against him.

"You," he begins, "take care of your friends."

I moan. "What did I do to deserve this? A little to the right," I coach him when one of his hands starts working down my back. "Mmm, that's it."

In seconds, he has me leaning against the table as he works down my back. "I should also tell you, I heard you the other day. Loud and clear."

I turn my head slightly. "You heard what?"

"When you were reorganizing the kitchen."

I glance off in its direction, curious. I recall a few days ago when I cleared out all the cabinets, restacked all the dishes, and sorted the glasses by type, size, and color. I was amazed at how many different sets of cutlery we had, and before I knew it, I was filling a box with fancy silverware and glasses we didn't need. "*I'm gonna sell them,*" I told Sam when he got home and saw the madness in the kitchen. I was in a bright blue tank top, dark blue jeans, and barefoot. "*We keep getting gifted these things we don't need. I could make a business of selling them on eBay! Or my own site!*" I told his befuddled face. *"I have it all sorted out in my head. I just need to find a ... a ... what do you call those people? Web designer? Developer? ... Hacker?"*

Sam gives my back one last little rub, then returns to his seat and takes my hand. "Are you worried about money because of those pair of very botched deals I bitched about last week? Babe, we're doing just fine, you and I. It isn't—"

"No, no." I laugh it off. "I'm not worried about money. I know you're taking care of us. I'm—"

"So why try to start a business? All you need to do is have fun, enjoy your days, and just—"

"Don't you *dare* tell me to 'just be my pretty self'," I cut him right off.

Sam lifts his hands in surrender. "The words didn't even cross my mind."

I relent at once. "Good."

Sam's eyes draw down to my chest in thought. He looks troubled.

Then, after a minute, he asks me, "So why *are* you trying to start your own business again, babe?"

I frown. "Again?"

"You already forgot your professional gay pet-sitter idea you had a year ago?"

"Oh, man." I snort. "That was just a phase. Mr. Ho's Yorkshire Terriers *loved* me."

"And there was your graphic design stint ..."

I shrug. "I thought I made Wade's latest round of headshots look amazing. And he *did* land that next audition, by the way."

"Are you still unhappy, Dean?"

"What's this about?" I ask, totally bewildered. "What's with all of the interrogating?"

Sam stares patiently into my eyes, and I sit there in my chair, sunlight bathing the side of my face from the window, with a sinking feeling that my husband is buying none of my protests.

Something's missing from my life.

It's been missing for a long while now.

It's a great big hole in my heart I have been trying to fill for years. Whether it's an involved-enough hobby, or a side business, or going on a little adventure with Garret, or taking the boys out for a night at the clubs, or urging Sam to take me with him on a business trip, I'm constantly fighting to fill my life with that one, special thing.

"I'm not unhappy," I insist, ignoring all those thoughts. "I'm totally, perfectly content."

Sam studies me awhile longer, pensive, lost.

Then he puts on a smile as brazenly plastic as mine while rubbing my hand. "So you think this 'reclusive phase' of Garret's will last as long as his last one did?" Sam finally asks as he lifts his mug of coffee to his lips with his other hand.

He changed the subject. Good. "I don't think so," I admit. "He just gets in these moods where he doesn't want to go out with us. And y'know what? That's fine. He's allowed to have his space."

"I wonder sometimes if you're not actually a mind-reader," teases Sam. "You know your friends better than they know themselves."

"Do I?"

"It's obvious."

"You know," I say with a self-important smirk, "this is the only time in which I'm thankful to be two years older than the three of them. I feel like a 'mother hen' to them. It dignifies me with a certain façade of *wisdom*."

"Two years older, yet you appear five years younger." Sam's socked foot gently nudges mine underneath the breakfast table. "And that, babe, is no façade. You're the wisest man I know."

I nudge him back playfully with my own foot. "You're just saying that because you're horny this morning."

"Horny? How can you tell?"

"Oh, I don't know. Because I'm a mind-reader? Or … because you have the next three days off …?" I grin suggestively.

"Well, technically I may still get called away, depending if a certain deal goes through, but …"

"And whenever you have time off, you get this extra …" I slowly drag my foot up the inside of his bare leg. "… *pep* in your *step*."

Sam eyes me.

The devil's in my smirk as my foot reaches the fast-swelling crotch of his tight boxer-briefs.

"Don't tug the lion's tail," Sam warns me, "if you aren't ready for the roar."

"Is that what we're calling it?" My foot presses

into his crotch, my toes curling around his firming-up cock through the material and massaging it. "A roar? Are you about to *roar* for me, babe?"

He shuts his legs suddenly, trapping my foot.

It doesn't stop my toes moving, massaging his cock, which can't help but to flex and throb against my evil foot. "Do you think I've put too much into one night?"

Sam is adequately distracted, but still manages to say, "One night? You mean the double date?"

"The *not*-a-double-date, yes. I mean, we can do without the bowling, if that's too much." I mull it over, my foot still squeezing his cock through his underwear. "Or the third club."

"Third club?"

"It always takes three before you find the right groove."

"Is that so? Is that a proven fact?"

"We can call it that. The first two clubs are warm-ups, for sure. Oh, and then Leo is having a birthday bash, apparently, so we definitely have to—"

"*No Leo's*," states Sam, squeezing his thighs even tighter on my still-wiggling foot.

I shrug. "No Leo's then."

"But I do have an idea what we can do *now*."

I lift an eyebrow innocently. "Oh, do you?"

With that, Sam bursts out of his chair at once, grabs me up into his big arms, and carries me off.

A bedroom door is kicked open and slammed shut.

A Dean is dropped onto a bed caveman style.

A Sam towers over him with fire in his eyes.

Then two horny men become two sweaty men, and the rest of their long morning is lost to grunts, shameless moans of pleasure, and jagged breath.

GARRET

It's just another day in the office.

A day like any other.

I have an inbox full of complaint emails I must address. Quiet, half-awake coworkers sit in their own cubicles, completing their own inboxes.

But today, I have a little secret.

A little secret between my legs.

Just reminding myself about it makes my cock flex, struggling to swell in a tight, metal cage that so cruelly restricts it, denying me a man's natural pleasure of a simple erection.

I close my eyes and bite my lip, enjoying the feeling of self-dominating my own body.

This might be the greatest toy Jeremy has ever given me: the ability to torment myself.

It's like I'm my own dom.

And for a control freak semi-sub like me who has been accused (more than once) of topping from the bottom, this might be the perfect compromise.

"Garret Haines."

I look up at once.

Mr. Kevin Kingston stands before my desk in all his real-life, bodily might.

I didn't even hear him come out of his office, nor approach me at all. I was completely in a daze.

"Sir," I greet him, feeling so beautifully small and submissive under his shadow with just that one dumb little word.

"In my office." He turns and heads off, just the faint scent of his one-strict-spurt-of-cologne gently lingering in his departure.

I waste no time. I get right up from my chair and, like a puppy on a scent, I follow the broad and commanding backside of my boss in his fitted dress shirt that pulls on his shoulders in the perfect way, every inch of it ironed and smooth and strict even in its mere presentation. His shirt is tightly tucked into his navy blue dress pants, which look like they were stitched directly onto his body, and no other person on Earth can possibly fit into them and make them look better, even runway models. Even the near-gleam of his belt has a commanding presence about it.

Or maybe it's just the thousand dreams I have had of what a more creative Kevin Kingston might do with a belt like that—and me underneath him.

My cock swells and pushes to no avail.

Goddamn, this is a lot more torture than I was counting on.

I enter his clean, minimalist office and follow him to his desk. I only take my seat the moment he takes his, as if following some lost rule of chivalry.

Mr. Kingston gets right to the point. "I have a favor to ask you, Garret."

"Anything," I tell him, agreeing at once to any favor he could possibly ask, even before hearing a word of it. "Anything at all."

When his eyes meet mine, there is a firm and unceasing keenness in them.

And as if I'd forgotten, the memory of our recent revelation to one another surfaces at once.

He knows what I am.

And I know what he is.

Ever since that reveal, there has been a thick, iron-hard cord of sexual tension between us. And through it races an endless, electrical pulse of possibilities, as if anything could happen between us at any moment.

Even right now.

Mr. Kevin Kingston's face hardens. "There is a week-long conference I must attend. I leave early tomorrow morning and won't return to the office until the following weekend. Nine days."

Oh.

I wasn't expecting that.

Anticipating my beautiful boss in the office is half the motivation to come into work at all.

"Nine days," I affirm with a curt, dejected nod. "I see."

His face is blank as a stone when he says the rest: "And I will be requiring an assistant."

My heart stops.

I lift my eyebrows, glassy-eyed. "S-Sir?"

"An assistant," he repeats. "Are you free for the next two weekends?"

Free? Am I free?

What a curious question to ask a guy whose dick happens to be crammed inside a small metal prison between his legs.

Oh. He's waiting for my answer. "Yes," I exclaim, my heart drumming. "I'm free both weekends, sir. I'll gladly be your assistant." Then it hits me. "But ... what about my work? How will the email quota be met next week without me? I'm your top performer."

"Your coworkers will need to step it up and work harder. And it is *because* you're my top performer that I'm bringing you," he goes on. "You will be required to attend every meeting I attend. I don't want a single note missed. I'm expecting your full attention at all times for every one of these nine days. There will be no relaxing for you. This is not a vacation."

Goddamn, he knows how to lay it down. "Yes, sir. I understand."

"You will be compensated more than your usual pay. Do you accept the responsibility, Mr. Haines?"

My dreams are coming true before my eyes. "Yes, sir. I accept. I won't let you down."

"Good. I'll expect you to meet me at seven in the morning, not a minute late, downstairs in front of the building with your luggage. We will leave from here together."

My cock swells futilely in its cage as I choke out the words: "I will be there, sir."

[2]

It is late Saturday night.
The city streets are full of music, chaos, and laughter.
The boys, however, do not seem to be having a good
time—at least, not anymore.
Dean, Sam, Caysen, and Wade left the latest club
sweaty, sore-limbed, and slightly intoxicated. Wade
keeps trying to tell the others a story about a drunk guy
hitting on him in the bathroom, but Caysen interrupts
over and over with bold, drunken declarations of
wanting to kick the guy's ass, and how.
But let us rewind to earlier in the night ...

DEAN

I've been watching Caysen and Wade all night.

At the first club, Wade kept tugging on Caysen trying to get him to dance, despite there being next to no one on the dance floor. I stayed at the bar with Sam, who gave me these long, adoring stares that just melted me. The bartender shot us looks the whole time, likely trying to figure us out.

The next club on my little itinerary, we all got looser. A lot looser. Wade's shirt came off at one point. Caysen danced with him out of necessity—to keep guys off of him, if I had to guess. I finally convinced Sam to dance with me, too, and then we spent four songs dancing and eyeing other couples, trying to guess who was going home with whom tonight. We were having stupid, silly fun. Then that one perfect song came on, and all four of us went crazy on the dance floor together. The world became ours.

On the way to the third club is when the joy of the night unraveled into a pile of dollar-store yarn.

It began with Caysen making a remark about how guys at clubs are the worst lays, Wade responding with a question about how many guys from the clubs that Caysen has slept with, and his returning a, "I think my late teen years lasted a lot longer than yours," which made all our heads turn up in confusion.

Wade was annoyed, and his mood didn't improve.

The third club was half as big and twice as packed as the last one, and the air was thick, hot, and full of questionable odors. Wade began to act very strange, and Caysen remained at the bar sulking.

I turned to Sam and flatly stated, "This was a mistake, wasn't it," to which Sam only shrugged and flagged down the bartender, who ignored him.

At one point, Sam was yanked onto the thickly crowded dance floor with Wade, and it was just me and Caysen at the bar. I nudged the sulking brute. "Hey, man. You and Wade alright? You guys seem tense."

Caysen scowled at his vodka tonic for a second before eyeing the dance floor. Neither of us could see Wade or Sam from where we sat. "I thought we would be happier than this. I thought Wade was in love with me, too. I thought lots of dumb shit."

"It's not dumb shit," I assured him. "You guys just have a lot of … 'trial and error' to get through. You don't know how to be boyfriends yet."

"We practically already were before," Caysen spat back. "We always fought. Ever since back in our college roommate days. Most of the time, we can't seem to stand each other. Isn't that textbook true love?" he asked me cynically.

I got close to him and brought down my voice. "I don't know what true love is, man. I think it's one of those 'fun house mirror' things that look totally different for everyone."

"I fucking hate clowns."

"Also," I went on, ignoring his somewhat non sequitur, "I think you're forgetting how much you guys have fun together. You've got so many inside jokes, even *I* feel lost around you two at times."

Caysen continued to scowl at his drink, then eventually ditched it altogether, heading back onto the dance floor in pursuit of Wade. I slid his drink in front of me and finished it on his behalf, my half-lidded eyes tiredly observing the crowd.

That brings us up to present time.

You know, where everything goes *all* wrong.

After ditching that suffocating space of a club, the

four of us make our way to a specialty pizzeria I had looked up that none of us have gone to. It has a near five-star rating, and there's at least six different kinds of pizza I've been dying to try.

Sadly, we never make it to the pizzeria.

"Would you stop interrupting?" blurts Wade.

Caysen snorts. He's had eight vodka tonics too many. "Why? So we can keep hearing about how, how the, how some guy just fucking went down on you in the, in that nasty, that gross-ass bathroom?"

"He didn't go down on me! I didn't say that!"

"You were about to, probably." Caysen's eyes look like he's half-asleep. "Fucking club sluts."

Wade steps in front of Caysen, stopping him. "I was just trying to say that some guy came on to me while I was trying to take a piss, and then this other guy made fun of him, saying he was 'thirsty' for dick, and I was like, 'Well, I'm not interested, so ...'" He sighs. "*Why* are you looking at me like that?"

"Guys ..." I try to cut in soothingly.

Caysen can barely stand up straight. He shakes his head. "You've always had boys crawling all over you. You don't even, don't even know how much, how many times I have to ..." He blinks a few times forcefully. "I think working out has made you a cocky little bitch, that's what I think."

Wade's mouth drops. "A cocky little *what?*"

"Guys," I try again, stepping in between them.

"*Bitch*," Caysen throws over my shoulder at Wade. "That's what I said. Now you're all, you're all *hot shit*, and you—" He stumbles as he tries to get around the roadblock I've made of my spread arms. "—you don't *want* me anymore."

Wade grabs his own head, baffled. "What the fuck are you even saying, dude?"

"I'm saying I'm *out*. Peace, motherfuckers."

Caysen turns away and heads off, stumbling as he goes and bumping into people along the way.

Sam sighs, then pats me on the shoulder. "I'll get him home safely," he says, then goes off after Caysen.

Wade is left standing there with a perplexed, frozen expression on his face.

I put an arm around him, guiding him away. "He is wasted," I point out unnecessarily. "Just let it go. He's insecure and rambling drunkenly."

"But what if he really feels that way?" Wade drank almost as much as Caysen, yet doesn't show it, except for maybe in his eyes. "I didn't change when I started working out, did I?"

"You seem more confident. Not cocky. I think it's a good thing. Don't you feel more confident at your auditions?"

"Well ... yeah."

"I'm certain Caysen is proud of you. I'm also certain that he's confused. Maybe so are you." I pull Wade toward me more as we squeeze past a group of loud teenagers passing us on the narrow walkway. "You guys jumped straight into the middle of a serious relationship without warning. That has to be mentally jarring for both of you."

Wade shrugs, staring at the pavement as we walk. "I guess," he mumbles. "I dunno."

"What I mean is, you had no beginning."

"Beginning?"

He's always a bit slow on the uptake. I stop at the corner and turn Wade to face me. "What I'm trying to say is, you guys need a first date."

Wade blinks, as if the mere suggestion just slapped him straight across his cute, bewildered face. He doesn't even reply, stunned.

"This double date thing was wrong," I admit. "You guys need some time as a couple *on your own*. Do things together. Go places. But first, the sexy two of you need to go on a date. A real one."

The crossway light flashes on. Everyone on the corner starts to move. Wade and I, like debris in a rushing river, carry on across the street. We make the rest of the way to the train station in silence, and I give a mournful look at the pizzeria as we pass it by. *I'll come back for you*, I promise it.

An hour and forty-eight minutes later, Wade is safely dropped off at his place, and after a few text updates with my husband, we reunite at home.

"Goodness, what a night," mutters my husband as we get undressed in our bedroom. "Caysen was a complete mess. I practically had to carry him up the stairs and tuck him into his own bed."

I smile sleepily. "You're such a daddy."

Sam, in just his boxers, crosses the bedroom and stops me just as I drop my underwear to my ankles, catching me naked.

His hands grip my arms powerfully. "Babe," he growls, "it's taken everything in me to refrain from climbing all over you tonight."

I bite my lip and wiggle my eyebrows.

One of his hands reaches around and cups my ass, pulling my body against his. My cock is hard in seconds, throbbing against his solid thigh.

I moan. "You've got me in your hot hands."

"I've got you," he agrees toothily. "Now the question is, what do I do with you?"

I lick my lips, then open them to answer.

The house phone rings instead.

Sam and I turn.

I frown. "Who the hell would be calling at nearly one in the morning? On our *house* line?"

"Maybe Caysen." Sam eyes me. "I told him we would be up for a while if he needed anything."

"Aww, why'd you lie to him?" I ask teasingly.

Sam kisses my forehead, then pulls away and goes for the phone on the nightstand. He answers. "Hello, Mr. Addicks-Pine here."

I smirk. He's always so *formal*.

As Sam listens to whoever it is, I follow my own "horny initiative". Quietly, I move to the side of the bed right next to my husband.

Then I hook some fingers into his boxers.

Sam stiffens and peers down at me. "This is Sam Addicks-Pine." He eyes me, as if saying *not now*.

But his cock says yes.

I give his boxers—already loose and ready to come off—an encouraging tug.

Sam's semi-hard cock bounces free.

"Yes, he's my husband." Sam eyes me again more severely. "Oh, no need to apologize. Who's this?"

I give the phone a dismissive gesture. *I'll call them back*, I mouth at Sam, then playfully flick off the receiver as I grip his cock with both hands and wrap my lips around the head.

Sam grabs my hair, perhaps at first to hold me back. But his fingers soon curl, giving in, and I go to town on his hard, throbbing cock.

He doesn't pull away.

"N-No, it's okay, we're awake. But I-I'm afraid he's … he's … he's got his hands *full* at the moment."

I throw him a thumbs-up at the pun.

"Yes, sorry, too busy to chat right now."

Sam impressively maintains his composure while his hungry-hungry husband sucks him off.

"Is this an emergency? Or can he c-call—?"

I let go of his dick and grab his ass cheeks, pulling him against my face and swallowing him.

Sam's fingers clench in my hair.

"Is this a g-good number to get a hold of you? This one that came up? Or—*Mmm, God*—"

I don't relent. Quickly, it's become a game of whether I can get my husband off while he's on the phone.

"And your … *umph* … your name is …?"

He's out of breath.

My hand twists as I pull my mouth up and down the length of his thick cock. It grows slicker and slicker with every bob of my head, with every long, smooth stroke of my hand.

"Y-Yes," he breathes. "He'll c-call you back. Yes, thank ... th-thank you. No, really, it's okay. Night."

The phone slams down.

I release my husband's cock from the prison of my warm, wet mouth, then innocently look up his body at his dazed, emotional face.

"You're not gonna blow," I tell him, "until you are balls-deep inside your man, and *not* on the phone with whoever that was who calls us at one in the damned morning."

The hand he's got entangled in my hair slides down the back of my neck, his grip becoming more tender. "Babe ..." His dick bobs in my face. "It was a friend of yours from school."

"Oh, yeah? Which school? College or, God forbid, high school?"

"High school."

I give his dick an experimental stroke down its slippery length, causing Sam to buck and moan. "Interesting. And who was it? Please tell me it was the hot and cocky quarterback from the football team, deciding that he's gay after all these years and wanting my nuts."

"*She* ... said her name was Isabel. But she said you might've known her as Izzie ...?"

My hand stops in place.

My face freezes, too.

Izzie. Izzie Jacobs.

Sam notices my general petrification. A look of concern crosses his face at once. "Shit. What's wrong? Is she bad?"

I cast my gaze to the floor, too stunned to reply.

I can't tell him. Because if I tell him, then I'll have to reveal a hundred other things I never told my own husband, secrets I've kept all these years.

Why is she calling? And why now?

"Is she the bitch who used to make fun of your hair? Or is she the one whose brother was a dick to you on the track team? Or … or …"

I swallow it all down in three choked seconds, put my sexy face back on, and look up at his eyes. "Nah, none of those. Don't worry. I barely knew her. Can't imagine why she'd care to call me, to be honest. Haven't seen her since we …" *God, this hurts to lie to my husband like this.* "… since we graduated."

"Really?"

"Maybe she just wanted to catch up," I go on with a careless shrug. "Couldn't fathom why, since we …" My sexy mood is fading fast. I'm not sure I can keep this up. "… barely knew each other."

Sam nods. "Well, you might see her sometime this week, apparently. She said she just flew into town for business. Took the red-eye. Apologized for the hour."

There goes my face again, flattening with shock.

Sam crouches down, bringing his face level with mine. "Babe, I can tell something's wrong."

I force the stomach-turning emotions away one more time and face my husband. "Sorry. I think I have a sudden …" I let go of his dick and slouch on the bed. "My head is suddenly …" I gesture at it, waving my hand tiredly.

Sam quirks a dubious eyebrow, then sits on the bed next to me. "It's alright, babe. Let's just rest. It's late and we've had a long night."

"Yeah, that's it." I give him a smile that's deflated and anxious. "A really long night."

Sam isn't stupid. My dear husband knows there's something going on, but he doesn't press the matter. He just does exactly what I want him to: he embraces me with his arms, rubs my back, and kisses the top of my head with care.

And as he holds me, I stare at the crumpled up bed sheets over his shoulder, peering into their wrinkly white depths like a crystal ball. And I ask the spirits of the bed sheets why this ghost from my past is entering my life again—*and why now, of all times.*

GARRET

The morning flight was delayed.

The next one, too.

With each unexpected delay, Kevin Kingston grew moodier and moodier. I didn't know whether to be worried or turned on at the prospect of being punished for something completely out of my control. My boss certainly looked like he needed someone to punish for all of the annoying delays.

But Mr. Kingston is not an unreasonable man. In fact, I daresay he was downright honorable in the way he didn't blame me for the issues of weather, or whatever it was that caused the delays. All I know is that the flight we eventually took was over six hours later than was planned.

The flight itself was easy and painless.

Well, if you ignore all the sneaked glances I made of him in his seat, wondering what he was thinking while he focused intently on his laptop, ear buds crammed in his cute ears.

I kept aiming my laser eyes at him, desperate to know if he wondered about me as much as I wondered about him. My heart was at a constant racing pace the whole flight. I wanted to press my elbow against his, but couldn't muster the courage. I thought I'd get away with "accidentally" grazing his leg with mine, but it was no use.

I was clearly doomed to just sit next to him and stare miserably at the seat ahead of me.

The plane landed smoothly.

Then there were tons of traffic problems on the runway, forcing us to wait in our plane for nearly an hour before it was finally able to be brought to the terminal to disembark.

The traffic on the way to our destination hotel was even more monstrous.

The whole way, Kevin made eight separate and lengthy calls to different associates of his, explaining the unfortunate delays. He'd intended to arrive at a crisp, early afternoon hour. Now, he'd be lucky to arrive by midnight.

Both of us were exhausted. We'd suffered very long days. And I hadn't even had a minute of time yet to enjoy the fact that I was taking a special trip with my boss, the man of my dreams, the man who has ruined all other men for me.

And now, at long last, we arrive at the hotel.

I wanted to take it upon myself to carry both my and my boss's heavy and rather cumbersome luggage from the taxi, to the lobby, and even up to the room (to impress him, of course), but the ever-reliable bell service intercepts my efforts, taking our luggage away for us—*much to my dismay.*

The hotel is a fancy, high-dollar establishment where CEOs and presidents and (likely) occasional celebrities patronize. I'm afforded five minutes of awe as I take in the lobby, which itself looks like a palace. This is nothing like the downtown hotel in which Jock-Con took place.

Of course, that was back home.

This is a totally different city, miles and miles and cities and state boundaries away from home.

Away from everyone I know.

Except Mr. Kevin Kingston.

"This is our room," he states as we approach the wide, cream-colored door of 801.

I'm following my boss with my eyes so glued to the attention-grabbing, plump, commanding ass of his pants that I don't even hear the word "our".

At least, not yet.

The door opens to a large executive suite with floor-to-ceiling windows lining the far wall, the stars and the city in view. There is a long sectional couch, a wide wall-mounted TV, a table, a kitchen, and a large desk in the corner under a giant framed painting, all of it lit by cool-colored floor lamps and a few splashes of light whose sources seem out of sight somehow. A door to the side opens to the dim, moody bedroom, which holds a king-size bed and its own separate wall-mounted TV.

The bell boy leaves our luggage in a spot in the main room, is tipped, and then promptly dismissed. Finally, I show my devotion by quickly grabbing up my boss's luggage and carrying it into the bedroom, which opens into the bathroom—a rather extensive one, at that. As I glance inside it, my eyes stretch wide to accommodate the sight of a larger-than-life bathtub and a sleek walk-in shower with glass walls and a rainfall showerhead.

This suite is glorious and pure luxury.

"Here, sir?" I offer, unsure where to set all his luggage.

The floor-to-ceiling windows continue into the bedroom where Mr. Kingston stands, pensive and peering out the glass at the city below. He turns at my question. "Yes, there is fine."

I place one of his smaller bags on the bathroom counter, then rest his larger suitcase on an ottoman near the front of the bed.

Then I glance at my own sad little suitcase. I worry for a second that I might've under-packed. We're here for nine days, after all.

When I look up, I find Kevin still staring at me from the windows.

I swallow before I ask my next question. "Is my room down the hall, or … on another floor? I didn't see a separate room key."

"There isn't a separate room key, because we don't have a separate room."

I blink, confused. "I …"

Then it hits me.

Wait. Is he saying what I think he's saying?

"Are we …" I can barely say the words. "Are we sharing …?"

"Yes," he answers for me. "We're sharing this suite."

I look at the bed, wide-eyed, picturing us both cuddled up like lovers in the big, fluffy sheets. *No way. He wouldn't.* My heart starts to race. "Um … are we … also sharing the …?" I nod at the bed.

"Of course not," Kevin clips at once.

My face flushes instantly. *So embarrassing. Of course you're not sharing the bed with your boss, you fucking idiot.*

But where *am* I sleeping then?

This is the only bedroom in the suite.

I glance down at the dark hardwood floor, now forced to picture myself sleeping there instead, like a dog, uncomfortable, sore back, aching all night.

Fuck. *Why does one prospect turn me on as much as the other?*

"The couch should be suitable for you," Kevin explains simply. *Oh.* "It folds out into a bed that's nearly as comfortable as the real bed itself. I should know, I've slept on it."

He goes to these big conferences twice a year.

Perhaps he shared an executive suite before.

"I imagine it saves money," I blurt, desperately trying to save face after my vapidly dumb faux pas, despite my brain constantly tugging me in a sexual direction with everything. "To share a suite and, um, not get separate rooms for these nine days."

"The money isn't the issue," Kevin informs me briskly. "I'll need you close-by. Each day, we may be working late into the night. It doesn't make sense to get two separate rooms."

"Oh. Of course." I'm such an idiot. My face is so red, it's prickly. *Relax, dude. Just relax. Ugh.*

"Do you wish to unpack for me?"

His question throws me completely. Did I hear him right? "S-Sorry, sir?"

"Do you wish to unpack my things for me?" he repeats, his tone a touch firmer. "Hang my shirts and pants in the closet carefully? Place my other delicates in the dresser drawers?"

His other delicates, he just called them.

I'm pretty sure this is a boundary-crossing issue for normal boss/employee relationships.

But we are no normal boss and employee.

"Yes, sir," I answer him.

He studies me for a second, squinting.

Maybe I'm overdoing the "sir" thing a bit.

Regardless, he either seems to like it, or he's allowing my continued obsequiousness, because all he says is, "Very well. Unpack for me while I make some important calls."

With that, he leaves me in the bedroom. The next minute, I hear him in the kitchen speaking softly on his phone.

I'm left in the bedroom with his things, and a glorious view of the city, and a bunch of questions.

Now's not the time for answers, clearly.

After a breath, I open his suitcase and, piece by piece, empty it. It becomes somewhat ritualistic, handling each of his dress shirts like they're made out of goddamned glass. His pants are treated with the same regal care, each one hung precisely on its hanger to prevent a single wrinkle. Then I tend to his socks, undershirts, and finally, like a reward for all my day's efforts, his underwear.

Is my behavior still considered pervy if I think my boss is *expecting* me to have a strong sexual response to this task?

No matter, I take my time in placing each and every one of his "delicates" into the drawers of his dresser under the TV. Each is meticulously folded and thoughtfully organized. I am forced to imagine just how he might look wearing each and every pair of underwear I put away.

It is emotionally excruciating.

Maybe that's the point.

When I pull out his last pair of underwear, I'm given pause. Great and terrible pause.

It's a pair of shiny black compression shorts. Like, for an athlete. It's complete with reverse stitching that draws a curved seam down both sides of the ass. The waistband is thick, high-contrast black and white, with the brand name in big block letters: *JOCK FUCK.*

What the hell kind of brand is that?

It doesn't matter. It has the intended effect of obliterating all my senses. It makes me see Kevin Kingston in full football gear, head to toe. *He was probably wearing this underneath all that gear at Jock-Con. This matches his whole color scheme.*

This is a message, that's what this is.

This is why he wanted me to unpack his things for him, so that I would find this.

I sneak a glance through the door. Kevin is still in the kitchen, his back turned to me, speaking in a cool, humorless voice to someone on his phone.

While watching him, I slowly lift those tight, shiny, black compression shorts to my face.

And inhale.

Deeply.

Of course it's washed. Pristinely. Only laundry detergent aroma fills my nostrils, not the delicious, manly scent of Kevin himself. But just the feel of that slinky, tight material against my lips, my nose, and my cheeks is enough to drive me fucking nuts.

Then, with a resigned sigh, I fold them up, too, and slip them into the drawer with the others.

Message received, Mr. Kevin Kingston.

He's still on the phone by the time I finish, so I grab my own suitcase and quickly unpack in the remaining bottom drawer, which I assume will be alright with him, as I have nowhere else to put my things. Then I move all the emptied suitcases into the closet, shut it, and stop in front of the bathroom mirror to stare at my face ponderously.

My eyes glide down to my crotch.

And a nearly undetectable bulge caused by a tiny, dark secret of mine.

Yes, sir. I'm still wearing it.

Yes, sir. It made stuffing my nose into my boss's sexy, athletic compression shorts that much more erotic—and uncomfortable.

My dick wants to get hard so badly that it's throbbing right now, confined in its little cage.

It was a bold—and perhaps reckless—decision I made back home when I packed. I had the key in my hand and was seconds away from unlocking my cock cage and freeing myself.

Then, as my horny mind always wins and takes precedence over all my senses, I told myself: *You'll never have this experience again. Kevin is about to own you for nine consecutive days. You will be around him all the time, serving him, assisting him, and being his little helper toy.*

Did I *really* want to let my cock out? Or did I want to extend my self-imposed punishment, and therefore my pleasure, by keeping my precious dick trapped in this tight, confining thing?

I bit my lip, felt a stroke of evil, and pocketed away the key.

My decision, however, cost me a minor heart-attack at the airport.

Y'know, when I went through fucking security.

And belatedly remembered with a start what I was wearing in my pants.

I was terrified in that long line. Kevin glanced at me once or twice, as if wondering why the hell I was fretting and fidgeting and breathing so much. I couldn't help but squirm anxiously in silent terror, wide-eyed and dry-mouthed, as we approached the TSA agents.

Then it was my turn to do the thing.

I took a breath and stepped forward, every part of my body trembling, even my earlobes.

And a brief earful of beeps stopped my heart.

I don't know what came over me. But I gave that TSA agent a look, and out of nowhere, brilliance struck me: "I've got a Prince Albert."

The uniformed man quirked a strict eyebrow, glanced down at my crotch, then skeptically back up at my face.

And to my absolute astonishment, he responded: "You're the third *prince* I've met this past hour alone."

Insert: me gawping at him through my wide, frozen eyes.

And I was sent on through without any further problem.

True fucking story.

That is what I would classify as a proper *I-nearly-crapped-my-pants* situation.

Especially considering all the *"step aside and be strip searched and explain your dirty, shameful little self"* nightmares I had as I stood waiting in that line.

I mean, can you hear the five o'clock news? *This just in: Airport shut down on account of one horny homo and his dick toy.*

I wonder if people with actual private-part piercings are handled as easily.

And now, just about twelve hours after that close-call at the airport, and twenty-four hours after the reckless decision I made back in my safe, quiet home to keep my cock prisoner to its little metal cage, I stand here in this grand and glorious executive suite bathroom. Slowly, I slide my hand down into my tight pocket with a smirk.

My fingers touch the cold metal of that same wicked little key.

I stare challengingly at myself in the mirror. A smirk of secret pleasure curls my lips. *How long do you think you can keep this evil little game of yours going, Mr. Garret Haines?*

[3]

Monday evening rolls around with unseasonably thick
air, cloudless skies, and the scent of summer.
Caysen and Wade sit at a table in the middle of an
otherwise empty restaurant, save for one couple in the
corner who are sharing a candlelit volcano brownie.
Whether it's someone's birthday or an anniversary,
neither Caysen nor Wade can tell.
Also, neither of them could really give a shit.

CAYSEN

Our waiter is a young, doe-eyed twink whose gaze
keeps lingering on Wade each time he checks up on us.

It's annoying. *To say the very least.*

Not to mention how our little "first date" here is
going. The appetizer came and went, and Wade and I
had about three things to say to each other. Two of
those three things had to do with how tasty our stupid
fucking appetizer turned out to be.

The third thing was: "Do you think it's their
anniversary? That couple in the corner?"

To which I answered: "I couldn't give a shit."

And after a calm moment of reflection, Wade shrugged. "Me neither," he decided.

Then we fell quiet as our steak dinners arrived. Both of us medium rare, both of us with a side of vegetables, both of us with a chickpea salad.

Now here we sit in silence as we eat.

One short, awkward bite at a time.

While chewing, I look up at Wade and catch him looking at me.

He gives me a lift of his eyebrows and a slow nod, as if to say: *Yes, we're eating, how lovely.* Then he glances off.

I struggle to swallow my bite, suck a bit of meat out of my teeth, then look at him. "Is this really how our first date would've gone?"

Wade glances at me suddenly, surprised by my speaking at all. "Sorry?"

I point at our steaks. "Why is our first date full of awkward silence and nothing to talk about?"

Wade gives a halfhearted chuckle, then peers down at his plate. "I guess it's different when you kinda already know so much about each other."

"So how about we tell each other something we don't know?" I suggest. "Something new?"

Wade appears inspired for a moment, coming along for the ride. "Like what?"

"Like … hey, tell me, when was the first time you snuck out of your parents' house to go hang out with your friends?"

"I never did."

"Oh."

After a moment, Wade cuts a bite off his steak, slips it past his lips, then chews as he stares at me.

I set down my fork and knife.

It isn't the date that's awkward. It's me. And it's Wade. And it's something between us that I've been avoiding bringing up this whole time.

"Wade, I'm ..." I sigh. "Listen. I'm still sorry about all of that shitty stuff I said to you. A couple nights ago. The stuff I said after all those annoying clubs Dean dragged us to."

Wade lifts his eyebrows lightly. "*Still* sorry?" He makes a face as he strikes his next bite with his fork. "Didn't know you were sorry to begin with."

I frown defensively. "Of course I was sorry. I said I was. And I still am. I'm sorry right now."

Wade's eyes harden. "And?"

I shrug. "And what?"

"Is that all you're apologizing for?"

I return his hardness with a long stare of my own. I guess I deserve this. "Alright. I'm ... sorry for being a dick in general."

"And?"

"And ... I'm also sorry for starting this whole 'boyfriends' thing off in such a shitty way. I'm not really used to it, in my defense."

"And?"

For fuck's sake. I'm at a loss. "What else did I do, Wade? I was a dick. I got drunk and turned into a big dick. I *told* you I never drink, and it's for a reason. *Other than alcohol is the worst thing you can put into your body, by the way*," I add quickly. "What else are you wanting to hear?"

He shoves another bite of steak into his mouth, then speaks while he chews aggressively. "You know exactly what else."

My eyes detach as I think it over. Then I throw my tired eyes at him. "Dude, I have no idea what else. Just tell me."

Wade glances down at his plate as he cuts another bite. Then, only after popping the juicy morsel into his mouth, chewing it, and swallowing, he finally asks, "Do you really not remember the stuff you said to me that night? Specific stuff?"

I was hoping I wouldn't have to acknowledge how much of a blur that night was. I can't recall any of the words that flew out of my mouth.

"You said I'm too cocky," Wade starts.

I screw up my forehead. "Too cocky?"

"Ever since I started working out. You said I think I'm hot now and it's making me cocky. You also acted possessive all night, becoming *furiously* jealous of any guys who came near me, even on a crowded dance floor. You nearly started two fights."

"Did you *see* them?" I protest in my defense. "Those dudes wouldn't leave you alone, and half of them were tweaked off their asses."

"It's like you think I'm gonna go find someone with my 'new hot bod' now." Wade laughs at that. "I didn't become some sex god overnight, Cays. I barely see a difference when I look in the mirror."

"Are you kidding?" I gesture at him. "It's like night and day with your confidence. You're bolder. You walk taller. I notice these things."

"Is that what this is all about?" His tone shifts suddenly to something softer. "Is that why you've become so insecure? You think—"

That word sets me off. "I'm *not* insecure."

"—that one day I'm gonna respond to one of these dudes hitting on me? That I'll take one of them up on an offer because I'm so 'hot' now? What the hell kind of guy do you think I am?"

I cross my arms. "You're sometimes naïve."

"Oh? Am I?"

"Yes. And oblivious. You need me to protect you," I point out. "I'm not being possessive or ... or ... or whatever you're accusing me of. You need a guy like me who takes no shit, a guy who'll see things that you don't always see."

"I have a different hypothesis." Wade's eyes turn sensitive. "Maybe now that you've admitted your feelings to me, and we're trying ... *whatever this is* ... you suddenly have something to lose."

My eyes drop to the table.

Wade's hand shoots around both our plates like a ninja and takes a gentle hold of mine. I fight a stubborn instinct to yank it right back and insist I'm alright and don't need my hand held. Instead, I allow him to hold it, staring at our gripped hands with iron-hard focus.

"I told you, Cays, nothing between us needs to change, and I meant it."

His voice is so soft and warm and kind. He's more of a man than I'll probably ever deserve.

But I've known him a long time. And Wade, of all the friends I've ever had, is the most skilled in the art of denial. Despite his good intentions, he's not always honest with himself.

I lift my chin and peer into his face. "Even you don't believe that, bud."

Wade's eyes falter.

There's a presence at our side. The twink of a waiter we have stands there dutifully, his gaze on Wade, full of dreams and wishes and whatever. "Are you two enjoying your dinner?" he asks.

I look up at him. "Obviously," I answer curtly.

The waiter glances between us, eyes wide, then bows away from us, disappearing somewhere.

When I turn back to Wade, I find his eyes narrowed. He smirks. "Was that necessary?"

I shrug. "The fucker won't leave us alone."

"I needed a refill of water, as a matter of fact. It's his job to not leave us alone. He's our *waiter*."

"And you're a delicious dessert that isn't on the menu."

Wade appears to exercise patience as he burns a hole in my chest with his eyes.

My temper ebbs like the tide, staring at Wade's fierce eyes. "Just tell me."

Wade lifts his eyes to mine. "Tell you what?"

"Tell me what I'm doing wrong. Tell me what you want me to do differently. I'll do it."

He studies me for a moment, clear skepticism in his eyes. Then, rather quickly, a hint of humor twists his face. "Well, maybe you can treat me a bit rougher in the bedroom."

I quirk an eyebrow, surprised.

I wasn't expecting that.

Wade eyes me. "I'm not some delicate fuckin' flower." He smirks suggestively.

I nod slowly. "Alright, noted. Rougher. And what else?"

After another minute of looking me over, he says, "And stop freaking out all the time. We can be buds, just like we were. Except we're also ..." He shrugs, thinking of the right word to choose.

We're still holding hands. I give his a squeeze, pulling his attention back to me. "Maybe change can be a ... *good* thing."

Wade peers down at our hands. Then he seems to come to a decision. "Maybe it can."

The couple in the corner laughs at something, maybe a joke that was told, or something silly one of them said. But neither Wade nor I seem to give a shit, too drawn into our own moment here to afford them even a glance.

Wade gazes thoughtfully at our hands awhile longer before he speaks. "I'm always surprised by your soft hands. With all your weightlifting, you'd expect them to be rough and calloused ..."

I let my thumb graze gently across his skin. He moves his fingers slightly in response, stroking the inside of my palm.

Then he lifts his eyes to mine.

My gaze drops to his lips.

As if chasing the same instinct, we lean across the table at once, and our lips gently touch.

GARRET

We return to the hotel room after attending our last conference of the evening.

Finally.

Kevin sets down his briefcase on the desk, pops it open, and starts to organize his things. As if already used to Kevin's very particular routine, I fetch his tablet and laptop without being asked to, sit down on the couch, and begin the long task of transferring my notes from the tablet onto a bunch of spreadsheets on the laptop. Neither of us speak; we just attend to our duties like we do this every day. For a while, the room is silent except for the soft sounds of our respective typing and item sorting.

From the desk, Kevin breaks the cool silence. "Are you hungry?"

I look up and quickly wipe the weariness out of my eyes. It's probably only eight or nine right now, but after the long and grueling day we've had, it feels like well after midnight. "I'm ... I'm fine."

"I'll treat us. What do you like? Any preferences?"

I freeze. Should I have any? Should I decline? *Why does everything feel like a test with him?* After a quick calculation, I realize it's probably more respectful to accept his offering. "I'll take whatever you're having, sir. I'm fine with anything."

Kevin studies me. "You like calling me that?"

I stare at his completely unreadable face across the room. "Sorry?"

"'Sir'. You call me 'sir' all the time. You like to call me that?"

Already, my heart is thumping desperately. A restrained organ between my legs is starting to fill its tiny metal home, fighting against its walls.

"I ..." Do I go for a sexual answer, or a logical one? "I ... try to be respectful to my ... s-superiors."

"Your superiors?" His voice is even and firm. He carries no hint of mockery or sarcasm when he repeats my words back to me. "Is that how you see me, Mr. Haines? As your superior?"

I stare at him. "You ... *are* ... my superior."

"But right now, we're essentially off-the-clock. We're in the hotel room. The next conference isn't until ten o'clock tomorrow morning. You and I are free to be human beings until then, are we not?"

Free?

To be human beings?

Is he implying something, or is this all literal?

"Of course," is all I can manage to respond.

"So my point is, if you want to call me simply Kevin during our 'off time'," he explains, "I think that would be acceptable."

I nod. "Yes, sir." I flinch. "I mean, yes, Kevin. That sounds … reasonable."

"Good." He picks up the phone off the desk, taps a button, then brings it to his ear and orders us a pair of sandwiches. His tone carries such steely authority that I'm left just staring at him, clinging to the strength in his voice, and feeling …

What am I feeling?

Satisfied? Included? Attended to?

I guess it doesn't really matter. Whatever it is I'm feeling, it's left a thought-filled smile on my sleepy-eyed face.

I'm the luckiest little employee of anyone in the world that ever lived.

But while staring at him, something else creeps slowly into my mind, like a giant cloud swimming over my sunny field, casting it in shadow.

He knows my secret.

I know his.

Why are neither of us acknowledging the very thing we both know about each other, the thing that makes our relationship so unusual, so special, so particular?

The only semblance of "gear" that he packed was the one I buried my face in.

Why else did he make me unpack his things, if not to find those sexy compression shorts? Why'd he put an idea into my mind, only to sexually ignore me? *Not that we have much time for playing anyway, with all these back-to-back meetings.*

But he just now made the point of having me call him Kevin in our "off time". What's the point of that? To put me at ease? To comfort me?

Or …

Or to tell me he isn't interested in me. He isn't interested in fulfilling any of my fantasies. He brought the shorts for himself, in the same way I'm wearing a cock cage: just for myself.

Maybe I've had it all wrong.

Kevin hangs up the phone so abruptly, I jump. "The sandwiches will be here in fifteen to twenty minutes. I'm going to take a shower. Need to use the bathroom before I occupy it?"

His question, even politely as it's worded, has that all-familiar tone of authority in it. If I was a man who didn't feel the way I did about Kevin, I'd think his voice was arrogant, haughty, or snobby. Instead, I find it irresistible and perfect.

And I do have to pee.

Somewhat badly.

But instead, I say: "No, sir. I'm fine."

Kevin nods at me, then dismisses himself.

The bedroom door shuts. Then, within, I hear the bathroom door softly close, and the water runs.

And I stare at that bedroom door thoughtfully, wondering whether I'm right or wrong, whether Kevin wants me or doesn't, whether this is all for nothing—

all while holding my pee like a good, pent-up, stupid boy who never learns.

I peer down at the tablet and the laptop. With a resigned sigh, I resume my tedious work.

DEAN

After checking my phone for the seventeenth time, I squint at the wall where a slim digital clock reads, in bright green letters: 10:14 PM.

Fourteen minutes late. No big deal.

She doesn't live here. Everything is unfamiliar. She'll likely be late, navigating the subway, or the taxi, or however she's choosing to meet me.

When 10:36 PM rolls around, I wander away from the aromatic deli and into an attached arcade next-door. The colorful lights and noise assault me, yanking me back into the 90s when I used to hit up arcades all the time with my friends. I find myself standing in front of a classic Ms. Pac-Man, smiling blankly as the little yellow gal eats up all the tiny dots. Even though it's just the demo playing, I cheer her on in my mind, urging her to avoid the ghosts. *No, no, the pink one is coming right around the corner, no, no, stop, turn the other way, stop!*

Ms. Pac-Man gets eaten.

I pout. No one ever heeds my warnings.

"Dean?"

I spin around toward the voice.

What a sight she is. Even after ten years of not seeing her, Izzie Jacobs looks just the same as I remember her. Wavy brown hair, but cropped at her shoulders now. Cute, pointy nose. Lips that form a perfect, plump heart. Astonishingly sharp green eyes. She's an absolute doll.

"Izzie," I greet her, a tentative smile spreading over my face. "Wow. You … haven't aged a day."

"And you're married to a man!" she returns just as daintily.

My smile falters.

She tries to laugh it off. "Sorry. I'm still … I'm still processing the whole Addicks-Pine thing."

"Right. No longer just Dean Addicks." I return her laugh with a choked chuckle of my own. I can't stop looking her over, surprised she's actually here. "You must've been, uh … caught off-guard when you called my house and … and my lovely husband answered the phone." I wipe my hands on my pants, realizing they're sweaty. I feel like I'm about to ask her to prom or something.

What the hell is up with my nerves?

"I mean, I'd heard a few things over the years. I won't lie," she goes on, "but … well, still."

I lean against the Ms. Pac-Man. "What *have* you heard, exactly?"

Now it's Izzie who looks caught off-guard. "I just heard, um, well …" Her face adopts a look of sudden courage. "I heard I turned you gay."

I have to stare at her for a solid ten seconds to be sure she isn't kidding.

"That's ... not how it works," I slowly say.

"I *know that*," she retorts laughingly. "That's what Brett and Emily said. They have small minds. Tiny minds. You have to just shrug it off."

"To be fair, if I *was* out back then, I'd have been the only *out* gay guy for fifty miles in any direction you throw a stone," I remind her.

Her smile looks like a grimace. "True."

"That's the first reason on a list of about fifty of why I moved here away from our small town."

"Was I one of those reasons?"

Her tone hardens with that last question, yet carries that all-familiar lilt of innocence with which she's spoken ever since we were just two fools whispering to each other in the back of Ms. Mortimer's English class.

I shake my head. "No, Izzie. You weren't."

"We broke up rather quickly." She inspects her fingers for some reason. "After three long years, graduation came and went, and suddenly you just had to ..." She lets out a short huff. "... end it, rip off the Band-Aid, no discussion at all."

I frown. "That's not how I remember it."

"Oh?"

"We mutually agreed to end things. We were going to schools on opposite sides of the country. There's ..." I'm uncharacteristically defensive at once. "There's no way it would've worked out. We both agreed about that, didn't we?"

Izzie shrugs, then crosses her arms. "Well, I guess we can agree to disagree on exactly how that particular conversation went."

I deflate, staring into her eyes with sadness. "I'm sorry if I hurt you, Izzie."

"I am, too." She looks away.

The Ms. Pac-Man music plays in my ear over and over as I stare at Izzie. A sudden bolt of worry surges into me. "Why are you here?"

Izzie doesn't look at me. She stares off at a pinball machine for a bit, arms still crossed, before finally answering, "I ... wanted to see who you are now. Who you've become."

"Really? C'mon, Izzie. That isn't a reason to take a red-eye all the way out here. Unless this is about to turn into some low-budget made-for-TV horror flick about an obsessed ex-lover who ..." A flick of her annoyed eyes tells me this joke I'm making isn't appreciated. "Sorry, Iz. I'm not calling you an obsessed ex-lover. That was dumb. Just tell me the real reason you came all this way. It isn't just to see who I am."

"But it is," she insists. "I wanted to see for myself if you ..." Her eyes graze down my body. "If you've really changed so much."

"I'm Dean. The same Dean you knew. Just ..."

"Gayer?" she offers coolly.

If I'm being completely honest here, I'm not sure she's as gay-friendly as I always pictured her to be in my head. For all I know, she's disgusted with me and my husband. I have no idea what the world's done to her over the past ten years. People change. People's beliefs and politics change. It's no telling who this woman is who's standing in front of me right now.

I push away from the Ms. Pac-Man and come in front of her. She looks up at me. "Izzie ..."

"I'm sorry," she says suddenly, her eyes wet and her face collapsing into something of a wince. "I had no right to just ... burst back into your life like this with all these swinging accusations and interrogations and—*Augh* ... I'm so awful."

"No, no." I reach out my hand to hug her, think the better of it, then just resign to a soft, awkward patting of her shoulder. "You're not awful."

"Yes, I am."

"No, you're not."

"Yes, I ..." She shuts her eyes, frustrated for all of two seconds, then flaps them back open. "We were supposed to meet at the deli. Are you hungry? I'm hungry. Let's get something to eat."

I force out a smile. I'm so not hungry anymore. But I make myself agree with her anyway: "Let's get something to eat, then."

Forty minutes later, we've eaten a pair of tasty sandwiches, and are each lazily sipping a tall cup of Cherry Coke. (It was our thing back in the day.) Both of our nerves have clearly eased over the near hour we've spent rambling on about nothing at all, reminiscing, sharing stories of our lives, and being totally sober idiots.

Motherfucker, I could really use some wine.

"You were my first kiss," I suddenly volunteer.

She gawps, surprised by that. "I thought you'd been with Rebecca Keesler! The volleyball girl!"

"That was, like, eighth grade, and yuck."

Izzie laughs too hard at that. "Wow. Maybe I knew that already and just forgot. How weird!"

"Isn't it?"

"And you didn't—?" She stops herself, unsure whether to ask the question, then visibly seems to say '*Ah, what the hell?*' and finishes her thought: "And you didn't know you were gay back then?"

My arms are crossed and resting on the table when I shrug. "It's a little complicated. I always felt different than the other guys."

"The guys on your track team?"

"Sure, and my other friends. I noticed the way they'd ... *brag* about their female conquests. The way they talked about banging Sheila, or Tabby, or *Laura-fucking-Langley*," I add with an eye-roll.

Izzie's chuckle she returns is halfhearted, as her full attention is on the rest of my answer, still waiting for it.

I go on. "I just never put two-and-two together until I went to college. Then I met a guy ..."

"Your husband Sam?"

"No, no. That came much later. I've had about four or five serious boyfriends. The first was a *complete and total train wreck*. He finally decided he didn't want to date a guy who was fresh out of the closet—or 'possibly experimenting'. I wasn't. I knew after him that I was definitely into men."

"Fascinating."

The somewhat flat way in which Izzie says the word "fascinating", I can't quite tell if she's being sincere, or masking an avalanche of emotions she won't dare spill in front of me.

"I've never really ... fit the 'gay mold'."

"Do any of us really fit our molds?" Izzie asks with a wistful smile. "I certainly don't fit an Ivy League graduate's mold by any means—working two jobs, can't keep a boyfriend, single mom ..."

"Single mom?"

Izzie's eyes turn into two stunned needles. "I meant I ... I was ..." She closes her eyes. "Yes."

I gasp. "Wow. Why didn't you tell me? That's amazing! Congrats, first off. And is it a son or a daughter? How old? Fuck the loser dad," I throw in. "If he didn't want to stick around for the kid, it's his loss. Oh, unless he died," I add suddenly, shrinking. "He didn't die, did he?"

Izzie shakes her head slowly. "No."

"So is it a son or a daughter? What's their name? Tell me everything."

"Son." She opens her eyes and offers me a tiny smile. "His name is Derrick."

"Did he ... come here with you?"

"He's at the hotel. Probably asleep."

I blink. "In a hotel all by himself? He can't be that old."

"He's with my sister. You remember Janie?"

"Oh, how could I forget?" I tease. "Does she still hate me? She was *relentless* when we broke up that summer. I still have the scathing emails."

Izzie lets out a nervous chuckle through her tightened throat. Then she casts her eyes down to her now-empty cup, fiddling with it. "She's been my rock through quite a lot."

"Oh my God, we should all hang out," I blurt out suddenly. "All three of you, me, and Sam. Hey, I can host a game night at my house! It'll be—"

"Dean …"

"It'll be so much fun! How long are you in town for? We all could—"

I grab my stomach at once, feeling a very ill-timed lurch. The table spins, the room shrinks, and all I can see is my crumpled up ball of delicatessen paper that once held a sandwich.

Oh, fuck.

Izzie leans over the table, concerned. "Dean?"

"It's …"

My "gut feeling" thing. A strong one. A very, very strong one. Strongest I've ever had.

What is it trying to tell me?

I look up at Izzie, my high school sweetheart, the one who was my companion through the best and toughest years of my life. And suddenly I feel my pulse in my neck, my stomach is performing a trapeze act, and fear is coursing through my body so potently I can feel it in my toenails.

My gut feeling once saved my and my friend's

lives when I insisted that we not take a subway home. The next day, we learned someone had been shot and killed on that very subway train around the same time we would've been aboard.

Of course, I've had a hundred of those same feelings ever since, and not one of them has saved our lives.

But this one isn't like the others. It's strange.

Is it telling me that this game night is a bad idea— or an absolutely necessary one?

Should I bother listening to it at all, for all the times it's let me down?

I'm not some kind of psychic. I'm not a special celebrity medium who needs a reality show to show off my gift. I'm just a regular neurotic guy with some weird pseudo superstitions.

Finally I make myself smile at Izzie across the table. "Indigestion. From the ..." I glance down at my cup. "... Cherry Coke. I gave up soda centuries ago. Maybe my body thinks I'm poisoning it."

"Oh. Sorry."

"Well, it's not like it's your fault," I tease, still clutching my stomach like it might run away.

"Does he know?" she asks. "Sam? ... About us?"

My eyes meet hers.

Something sensitive yet dark crosses her face when she notes my silence.

I lick my lips, then softly shake my head no.

Izzie sits back in her chair and lets out a sigh. "Well, that's something," she mumbles.

"It isn't that I don't *want* to tell him about us. I mean, I could." This is so hard to articulate for some reason. "It's just that I don't ... I don't want him to be *confused*. He's got a lot of insecurities. He thinks he's not enough for me. He keeps encouraging me to go out and have fun and sleep with younger guys."

Izzie looks taken aback by that.

Perhaps I need to remind myself that she isn't used to any of this, and I need to put on the brakes. I'm going way too fast. "Sorry. It's just—"

"How much older is he?"

"Oh, just a *feeew* years," I answer coyly, smirking. "Enough for him to think he's 'stolen my youth' by marrying me."

"So he doesn't ... know ... anything ...?"

I take a deep breath, then let it out with: "No."

"What are you, exactly?" She struggles with the question, like it's difficult to even say. "Are you bisexual? Or are you completely gay now?"

"I really don't think slapping a label on it is the answer," I start to say.

Her eyes harden. "Well, I think it is."

"Izzie ..."

"We took each other's virginity, Dean. That ... might be a little no-big-deal thing to you, maybe even a joke—"

"You're *not* a joke."

"—but what am I supposed to do with this new Dean sitting in front of me? And now you want me to come over and play games with you and your husband?

I mean, I don't even know who … who or … or what you've …" She shuts her eyes and buries her face with her hands, sighing.

I watch her for a while, bubbling over with a feeling that's lost in a cornfield of compassion and guilt. I'm not sure how to approach this with her.

So I dive straight into honesty land. "I lied to my husband."

Izzie lifts her face out of her hands, bringing her tired eyes onto mine and listening with caution.

"I was afraid. In much the same way I didn't know how *you'd* react to my being gay, I don't know how Sam will react to my not being a gold-star gay."

Her face wrinkles. "Gold … what?"

"It's a term. A gay thing. If you've never slept with a woman, you're called a gold-star gay."

She processes it, then sighs out a, "Alright."

"It's a stupid term," I blurt out at once. "I don't know why I said it. It's so gross and laced in sexist and heterophobic overtones, as if touching a vagina in any way makes me less of a gay man. They even have 'platinum-star gays' who were C-section birth babies and have *literally* never touched a vagina. Is that not the stupidest thing you've ever—?" I shut my eyes, quashing out the idiotic subject, and now doubly worried (judging from her off-put reaction) that the gold-star thing was just more unintended salt to the wound. "Forget all of that. Sorry. My point is, I'm just afraid. I … I *was* afraid. I'm still afraid. I don't know a damned thing, Isabel."

She takes a second, then forces out a slightly pleasant sigh. "It's all very confusing, I agree."

"Yes, confusing."

"For both of us," she adds. "I shouldn't sound like I'm blaming you, really, for anything at all. I mean, we were young."

"We were young," I agree, grateful at once.

"And you're a good guy, Dean."

"Thank you."

"You were a good guy back then, too. You're ..." She seems to yield any attempt at blunt honesty. "You are ... probably a good guy now, even still."

I try for a smile. "I have my moments."

She returns my smile with a collapsed one of her own. "You always have."

"Let's try a hangout," I insist, wrestling against the stubborn beast inside me that bites and snaps its jaws and growls threateningly. "Just a little get-together at my place. No pressure. All five of us. Will you come to a little nothing game night this week?"

She seems to be wrestling a beast of her own as she studies me, worrying over my words.

"It'll be so much fun," I insist.

"I ... don't doubt that."

"We can catch up even more. I can meet your amazing son Derrick. Your sister can hate me all night and make snide remarks. I'll even let her win sometimes ... *maybe*. That's a hard *maybe*." I throw my hand across the table and take Izzie's, startling her. "Just say yes."

She stares at our clasped hands for a long and uncertain while. Then, with the tiniest voice, she peers up into my face and mutters: "Yes."

WADE

We were supposed to go out to a club next.

Instead, we end up at Caysen's.

"Dude, I don't know how you manage to keep everything so neat and tidy," I remark, surveying his living room. "My place is like an episode of *Hoarders* except no one comes to my rescue."

Caysen snorts on his way to the kitchen. "It isn't *that* bad. You're an actor. Aren't all 'creative types' messy?"

"Not all of us," I answer defensively, stopping by his kitchen counter. "Just most."

"Hey, I'm only repeating words you've said to me back in college." He swipes a card he had clipped to his fridge, then tosses it on the counter at me. "Wanna get married?"

I blink. "Uh, what?" Then I glance down at the card. It's a wedding invitation. "Oh."

He chuckles, amused by my reaction. "Don't know if you ever met them back in college, but Chuck and Randall are getting married."

Turning the card over, I see a photo of them, all dressed up and put together, wearing matching suits and big toothy smiles. "They were more *your* friends."

"Well, it's this coming weekend, Sunday, and I forgot. I'm allowed a plus-one." He eyes me. "Wanna be my guy? I promise we'll avoid the bar this time. I *insist* we do, actually."

I smile at him. "Sure. I don't have a show Sunday, so let's do it." Then I peer back down at the invitation, lost in about a hundred other thoughts that have everything to do with and nothing to do with marriage.

I mean, isn't that sort of what dating is?

A marriage *try-before-you-buy?*

"Want some water?" he asks suddenly, opening up a cabinet and pulling down two glasses from the top shelf. "Or tea? It's all I got. I'm not Dean, so I don't have any fancy wine or liquor."

I chuckle. "Whatever you're having."

When he pulls open his fridge to fetch his pitcher of cold, filtered water, the world becomes slow motion. Every sinewy, artful cord of muscle shows through his fitted blue t-shirt, his back muscles spreading like wings. Even holding the heavy pitcher of water in his hand, his bicep bulges like a baseball, thick and proud with all his efforts in the gym.

"Thirsty?"

I flick my eyes up to his. "Huh?"

He pours himself a glass of water. "Is water okay? Or you thirsty for something else?"

"Um …" *Fuck, I can't think straight.* "I'll have … I'm thirsty for what … whatever you're thirsty for. Water. Water is fine. Water's great."

He pours me a glass, then sets it on the counter. I sit on a barstool at one side while Caysen stands on the other. His eyes are on mine as he brings his glass to his lips, then partakes.

I bite my own lip and just watch.

His neck dances with his every greedy gulp.

I never knew one neck could have so many individual muscles. It's mesmerizing.

He sets down his glass and gives me a look. "You gonna drink any?"

"Yeah, of course," I blurt too quickly, laugh it off, then reach for my glass ...

And knock it straight off the counter.

The water spills all over Caysen's stomach and crotch. He backs away, startled, and the glass hits the kitchen floor.

"Oh, crap!" I cry out, tossing the wedding card onto the counter and rising to my feet. "I'm so sorry! I'm a ditz! Fuck!" I come around the counter at once.

The pair of us stare down at the glass.

I lift my eyebrows, surprised. "It didn't break."

Caysen looks at me, his hands still spread. In one, he holds his glass, still full. His tight blue shirt is soaked in the front, sticking to his abs like glue now, and the front of his jeans are wet.

Sopping wet.

I swallow as I look him over.

His eyes land on mine, and he gives me a little smirk. "I guess some things are ... less fragile than they seem."

Reluctantly, I nod. "I guess so."

Then he sets down his glass and, without any warning, peels off his tight blue shirt.

My eyes fall on his thick muscled chest.

His cascading hills of abs.

His small, perfect button of a navel.

"You got me wet," he teases me, then pitches his shirt at my face.

I'm flung out of my daze in an instant to catch it. Then, holding his balled-up wet shirt, I meet his eyes again. "Sorry about that."

"That's okay. Just need to ... dry myself."

Then he unzips his pants, slides them down his wide, meaty legs, and lets them pool at his ankles before kicking them off.

His kicked-off pants land near my feet. He stands before me now in a pair of black boxer-briefs, which glue to his form even more than his tight, wet, blue shirt did.

My heart bangs against my chest.

We've already had sex. Why am I so nervous?

Why am I feeling like this is *actually* a first date, and I haven't seen Caysen like this before?

I close my mouth, push my posture up, and put on my usual humored face. "Your stripping routine can use a bit of work."

Caysen chuckles. "Well, you'd better give me some pointers, then."

I let go of his shirt.

It slaps onto the tile, wet and loud as a spank.

Neither of us move, our eyes on each other's bodies across the small kitchen, which seems to grow smaller with every drawn breath.

"That kiss in the restaurant ..." I start.

Caysen responds with a grunted: "Yeah?"

I lick my lips, tasting our kiss again, feeling his breath on my cheek, his mouth against mine ...

He leans back against the nearest counter, then crosses his legs at the ankle and folds his big arms across his muscled chest. In just his underwear, standing like that, staring at me the way he is, he looks like a fitness model posing for some fancy, sexy kitchenware commercial.

I cross the kitchen in four short strides, taking care to step over the fallen glass. Barely a drop of water made it to the floor; it's all over Caysen.

I stop just in front of him, our noses inches apart, our eyes held hostage by one another's.

"How long have you wanted me?" I ask.

Caysen's eyebrows pull in ever so slightly. He doesn't answer, his eyes burning mine.

"In general, I mean. Is it a recent thing?" I go on, fishing. "Or did it start while I was with my ex several years ago? Or after I dumped him? Or was it before that?" I tilt my head and place my hands on the counter, one on either side of his body.

He still doesn't move.

"Or even earlier than that?" I ask. "The college days? Our dormmate days? When did it start?"

"Does it matter?"

His sudden reply surprises me. With my hands on the counter as they are, my face is practically upon his, our lips so close, just a flinch could turn this into a kiss.

My heart thrashes desperately.

My cock swells in the confines of my pants.

Caysen is more than just my best friend. He knows me better than anyone in the world. He's cussed out professors for me in the middle of class. He stood up for me when an ex tried to spread ugly rumors about me across campus. He once took care of me when I caught a bad cold during finals week, even going as far as to make chicken soup for me, and the bastard can barely cook Easy Mac when he tries. He makes every effort where I'm concerned, and I never bothered to see it until now.

Is it just Caysen who's had the crush, or was I ignoring feelings that were clearly there all along, as obvious as a slap to the face?

But I'm such a dense and oblivious fool that I mistook all his deep, sensitive caring for "just what best buds do for one another".

We've never just been best buds. We've been lovers all along. *Lovers with a different name.*

"No," I reply. "It doesn't matter."

Then I kiss him.

Caysen is unlocked the instant my lips touch his. He opens his arms right up and invites my whole body into them like a treasure, pulling my dry chest against his wet one.

Electricity chases its way through my body as I

give in to his forceful kissing.

It's almost too hard. It's almost painful.

Almost.

And somewhere in our impassioned kissing, I suddenly realize I love it that way.

One of his hands slides down my body, cups my ass, and pulls our hips together.

His crotch meets mine.

His dick flexes with a desperate, raging need.

I grab hold of his underwear and thrust them down, taking control.

Caysen grabs hold of my shirt and peels it up over my head, taking control right back. Then he presses me against the counter, reaches around me, and undoes my pants in a hurry.

The moment my clothes fall to the tile, I grip the counter urgently and press my bare ass against his stiffened, bare cock, groaning as I feel him against me, demanding what I want.

"Don't go easy," I tell him, out of breath.

Caysen hooks his hands underneath my arms and pulls my body against him.

His dick teases my crack, sliding everywhere. He's become a wordless beast, his dick exploring down below as he grinds it against my ass, slowly at first, but with force.

"I'm not fragile," I keep going. "I'm like that glass on the floor. I don't break. Don't go easy."

He shifts his position with a huff of hot breath on my neck, adjusting to get a better angle.

One of his feet hits the glass, sending it rolling across the kitchen carelessly.

Then there's a set of teeth clamping on my ear.

I buck my head backwards, resting it on his chest, or shoulder, or wherever it lands, gasping under the electric sensation of his teeth digging into my sensitive ear.

With every little nip, he casts electricity down my body.

He lets go. Then there's the noise of a drawer being yanked open, its rollers squeaking.

I hear a squirt, then the snapping shut of a plastic lid.

Wait a second …

When I hear the squelching of lube working up and down his dick, it's comical suddenly.

I turn my neck. "In the kitchen??" I throw over a shoulder. "You store a bottle of lube in the fucking—?"

The tip of his dick finds my hole.

I gasp, my words choked away.

But he doesn't enter; he slides past my hole, teasing me with his dick every time it glides by.

"Maybe on second thought," I say suddenly, a pinch of nervousness overtaking my horniness, "you *should* be a bit easy. I do still need to be able to walk tomorrow for my rehearsal, and—"

"You talk a lot," Caysen notes.

His dick finds my hole again.

This time, his cockhead slides right in.

I suck in a lungful of air so sweet, I could cry.

"Oh, fuck me," I cry out.

He slides in deeper. "That's what I'm doing."

"*Fuck, fuck, fuck.*"

"Yes, yes, yes," he growls back, rocking his hips, his dick sliding in and out, deeper with each thrust.

My hands slip suddenly, perhaps from spilled water still on the counter, and my face and chest go down, pressed flat against the surface.

Caysen presses a hand to the back of my head, pinning me down, as he fucks me harder and harder.

There is nothing romantic about this.

It's pure fucking animal sex.

None of my long, belabored late-night jerking sessions have ever made me feel like this.

Turned on. Used.

Slammed.

Fucked.

A jackpot with every charging of his dick deep inside me. He fills me perfectly, like his meat was made to fit in me and no one else.

My dick is swollen so hard, it aches.

Caysen hits that spot inside me over and over.

I'm overcome with an urgent need to get off.

Frantically, I slide my hand down to my own dick and jerk myself. My mouth is wide open and tasting the sweaty heat that's formed between us.

His hand presses my face down as he fucks me hard and tight.

I'm already close.

"C-Caysen ..." I murmur desperately through his

fingers that press against my lips.

"Wade ..." he grunts back.

Then I race past the threshold, unable to hold it in any longer.

Boom.

I let go, coming wherever my dick pleases.

Jet after jet of sweet relief empties from my body, releasing a flood of pleasure through me that feels so good, I could cry.

This is the definition of sweet, sweet relief.

Without missing a beat, Caysen slides right out of me, flips me over, then jerks over my abs as he lifts my face up off the counter, bringing my eyes right to his.

"Wade ..." he says to my face.

I'm still swimming in ecstasy—practically drowning in it, in fact—my lips parted, my eyes half-open.

Caysen's strong, sweaty, fierce face hovers in front of mine.

We are both in this moment together, fully.

"Do it," I tell him. "All over me. Do it."

"You want it?" he grunts.

"*Yes.*"

And he does it.

I feel his warm, wet relief like another glass of liquid, except this one spills down my front. I feel his warmth all over my abs, my dick, even a shot or two on my chest.

Then Caysen sighs with delight, lets out a choked chuckle, and collapses against me on the counter.

I'm right there with him, throwing my arms around his body and holding him against me.

Our naked, wet, sticky bodies remain there in the cool, silent kitchen, embracing with all our sex trapped between us.

Only the sound of our breaths fill our ears.

Then I slowly start to move my hands, rubbing his wet, sweaty back. I put a kiss on his ear, then on his cheek, and when he lifts his face from my neck to get a look at me, I meet his lips tenderly.

When he pulls away, a smile is in his eyes. It makes those sexy eyes of his twinkle, like they carry a cute little secret in them.

I look into those gorgeous, rich irises, curious, and I whisper a word, like a cute little thing I'm trying on: "*Boyfriend.*"

His smile reaches his lips at last. Then he nods gently with understanding. "*Boyfriend,*" he returns to me, whispered as softly and gently as Caysen's voice can get.

We kiss again, our still-swollen dicks pressed between our sweaty bodies. There's a warm, strong pulse throbbing somewhere down there, but I can't tell whose it is.

[4]

The mornings seem to arrive earlier and earlier when
Garret wakes up each day, his nights' hours stolen
from him so fast, he feels like he never slept.
Wednesday morning comes the quickest.
It is 7:28 AM, and poor Garret has a problem.

GARRET

The problem is: morning wood.

Every morning since I've been here, in fact.

And with each morning, it gets more and more
aggressive, and not lovely to wake up to.

Imagine somehow stuffing your finger into a
thimble, then trying to straighten it like an idiot.

Imagine somehow cramming your whole damned
foot into a shoe five sizes too small, and that shoe also
happens to be made of metal.

Let me introduce you to my dick this morning.

None of that shit compares.

I lie here on the big, luxurious couch-bed, praying
for my (sad attempt at) morning wood to calm the hell

down. I need to pee so badly, and that act isn't going to happen easily with my dick throbbing like this.

"Morning, Mr. Haines."

I flap open my eyes and sit up, startled.

Kevin is in the kitchen, fully awake already. He wears pajama pants, a t-shirt, and a robe, and he seems to be brewing coffee at the counter.

"Kevin," I greet him in my groggy morning voice, though my horny brain greets him as: "*Sir.*"

He nods at me. "It's going to be a long day. Be sure you've got everything you need."

Another long day.

Another day full of straining in my cock cage.

Another length of hours of physical anguish that, day by day, is losing the dark, secret pleasure it once had for me.

I'm sort of over it suddenly.

I just want out of this damned thing.

All of those fun, horny-minded fantasies have waned, and all I feel is tension and dick-bursting pressure down there.

And my incessant morning wood isn't helping.

So what if I only lasted five days out of the nine? Who cares. Sometimes, you have to know when to call it and forfeit the game.

Here I am, forfeiting.

While he's busy with the coffee, I hop off the couch-bed and silently excuse myself to the bathroom. After shutting the door, I hastily pull down my shorts, revealing my poor, tortured buddy, then pull open my bag to fish out the key.

I fish for it.

I fish some more.

Hmm, did it fall under something?

I start pulling out things from my bag—hair stuff, teeth stuff, toiletry stuff—and examine the whole inside in detail.

Still calm, I unzip the front pouch of the bag and fish around some more.

Nothing.

I look up at myself in the mirror, blinking.

"I'm not gonna panic," I tell my reflection.

Last night when I took my shower, I genuinely considered unlocking myself to give my "sensitive areas" a little bit of relief. But this thing is made for long-term wear and is shower-safe, allowing for cleaning, good hygiene, and blah, blah, blah—

Where the fuck is the key??

I set it here on the counter last night during my shower (and momentary indecision), then placed it back inside my bag after throwing on my comfy sleep clothes. I know I did. I must have.

I ... think I must have.

Relatively sort of sure.

Did you forget to put it in the bag? Did it fall off the counter and you didn't notice?

I look down at the floor, my heart racing. I get on my hands and knees—literally with my ass out and the stupid annoying fucking cage slapping back and forth between my thighs as I crawl—and examine all around the floor. I look behind the toilet. I peer under the sink. I even look around the foot of the bathtub, then inside the bathtub, then inside the shower and under the shampoo bottles.

I rise off the floor and stare at the mirror. My panicked, heavily-breathing face stares back.

Knock, knock. "Garret?"

I look at the back of the closed bathroom door, my eyes wide with panic. "Y-Yes? Kevin?" I answer in an impressively level *everything's-fine* voice.

"Are you getting ready in there? We need to be downstairs in forty-five minutes."

I swallow hard, staring down at my bag and all my things spread out on the counter.

My eyes land on the drain.

Please don't fucking tell me it fell down there.

"Yes, Kevin. I'm getting ..." It's so difficult to breathe suddenly. "I'm g-getting ready."

"Your clothes are out here," Kevin goes on, his voice stern, "and I didn't see you take anything in there with you. What exactly are you putting on?"

It's less about what I'm trying to put on, and more about what I'm trying to take the fuck off.

"Garret?"

I slip on my shorts, shove everything back into my bag, and take a deep breath. *It's probably just lost among your shit,* I reassure myself. *You'll find it. And worst case scenario, if you don't, you'll just have to wait until you're back home where you have the spare key in your underwear drawer.*

"I just need to pee, and I'll come right out to grab my … uh, my clothes," I call out, red-faced.

Today is going to be a very, very long day.

The day begins as all the previous ones did. We consult with an itinerary of scheduled meetings and events, hosted by different companies. Kevin discusses with me (it's really more of him talking at me and me just listening) which ones will be most beneficial to attend. A half-hour seminar on "giving with heart to the customer". A two-hour scenario-based role-playing workshop for issues in the workplace and ideal responses to them. Some other seminar on PR professionals.

I'm not as focused today. I can tell. I miss half of what Kevin says to me before we start heading to the meetings. During the first one, which is just a long and monotonous spiel about in-house versus outsourced complaint-mail responses, I stop paying attention. Kevin notices, nudges me with a, "Mr. Haines?" and I snap back to attention, red-faced. I'd missed five or so minutes of note-taking.

The next meeting, my foot keeps bouncing in place. You'd better bet Kevin notices that, too, and shoots me a severe look.

We don't break for lunch until nearly two in the afternoon because Kevin needed to attend some cleverly-titled boring thing about "de-sensitivity training" at 12:30. We eat a catered lunch in a small ballroom, and the whole time, I'm staring at nothing and thinking about nothing.

Nothing except where that fucking key is.

It's at almost five o'clock after we leave a long seminar about—*I've already forgotten*—that Kevin pulls me aside in the hallway. "Mr. Haines, are we all here today?"

"Yes, sir," I answer quickly, yet seem unable to meet his eyes, like I'm ashamed. "I'm here."

"Is something distracting you?"

Keep your head in the game. "Yes. I mean, no. Nothing is distracting me."

"We have three more meetings to attend, then we will return and order dinner from the room."

Though that sounds like heaven, I glance down at my tablet to check something, then frown. "But you have dinner plans with the CEOs of—"

"I'm canceling the plans."

I look up at Kevin. "Why?"

"Does it matter why?" he returns curtly.

I give it just a second's thought, then shake my head. "No, sir."

"Good. Stay alert for these final meetings. I won't tolerate any more missed notes."

He has my full attention suddenly. A second wind has found its way into my veins, invigorating me. I don't know how he does it. "Yes, sir."

And off we go.

Before I know it, my iPhone reads 8:23 PM, and the pair of us are entering the door to our hotel room after this long, exhausting day. And without fail, the pair of us go to our respective places—him at the desk, me at the couch—and we tend to our usual tasks of him organizing his things and me transferring notes to the company laptop.

I know the drill.

Also, I'm fucking starved.

My dick is mercifully soft right now, but just the notion that it's still helplessly trapped is, in its own way, a mental prison from which I clearly have not been able to escape all day.

It's in my every thought. *Where's the key?*

I'm reminded of it every time I look at Kevin, who is handsome and commanding no matter what time of day it is, no matter how he's dressed, no matter what has his full attention. *Where's the key?*

And I'm thinking about it now, sitting here on this couch, typing away on the laptop, tapping my fingers on the screen of the tablet, and trying to ignore the clunky, foreign object that's forcing my thighs to stay spread apart for comfort's sake.

Where is that motherfucking key??

"Garret."

I keep my eyes on the screen as I answer him. "Yes?"

"It's time to be honest with me."

His words make my fingers stop.

My gaze lifts to meet Kevin's across the room where he sits at that desk.

He's so damned good at just sitting at desks and looking important.

"About what, Kevin?"

He eyes me. "You've been distracted all day. I can't afford that same sort of distraction tomorrow, nor Friday, nor Saturday, nor even Sunday."

I nod quickly. "I understand. I promise I'll be on my game tomorrow."

"I need more than your promises."

"I … W-What do you mean?"

Kevin pulls open a drawer of his desk, plucks something out of it, then rises. He begins a very, *very* slow stroll toward the couch. "Tell me what's been distracting you all day."

I have no idea how I'm supposed to be any less distracted with my commanding boss doing that slow saunter toward me from his desk.

Hell, if he asked what my name is right now, I wouldn't know.

"Go ahead," he says. "Tell me."

"I …" *Well, if you must know.* "I … misplaced something."

"Did you?"

"Yes. I think I might've lost it somewhere in here." *He doesn't have to know what it is. I could be talking about a secret plush Pikachu doll I cuddle with at night.* "I was looking for it this morning."

"And it's valuable to you?"

I give him a coy look. "You can say that."

"It wouldn't happen to be …" He stops at the end of the couch, towering over me with his tall, imposing shadow. "… a *key*, would it?"

I snap my gaze up to him, alarmed.

Oh my God, he found it.

"Y-Yes," I state, keeping my voice matter-of-fact. "It is, actually. A key."

At that, Kevin opens his palm, revealing the item he pulled out of that desk drawer.

The key.

"Oh." I feign nonchalance and muted shock. "I see you've found it. What a great relief. Now I can unlock my …" I clear my throat. "… my apartment door. When I …" *Good Lord.* "… get home."

"This little thing is the key to your apartment?"

I'm so stupid-bad at lying. "Yes."

"This … tiny key … fits a full-size door?"

My eyes flick to it. "It's a … very small lock."

Kevin peers down at the key himself. He lazily pinches it between his fingers and inspects it with such slow and demonstrative attention, it feels like he's mocking my stupid answers.

He eyes me. "And you're telling the truth?"

"Yes," I blurt at once.

"You wouldn't lie to your boss?"

"No, I wouldn't, Kevin."

"I believe 'sir' is more appropriate right now."

My eyes shrink. My mouth is dry in an instant. My heart races so fast that my dick can't help but flinch in response, as if it's named and just heard it being called out loud and clear by Kevin himself.

I lick my lips. "I-I'm sorry, I don't follow."

Kevin tilts his head, studying me. "I think you might be underestimating your boss's knowledge of certain things. We did, after all, run into each other at a very specific sort of convention not too long ago, did we not?"

All of the blood rushes out of my head in a silent, sense-stealing sort of panic. I am literally incapable of a response or a reaction; I simply stare at him with my breath held and my lips parted.

Kevin gives the key one miniscule wiggle. "I happen to be very familiar with this style of key. And the style of lock it fits into. See," he goes on, his tone more casual and oddly personal than he's ever spoken to me before, "I happen to own several toys of my own that require certain keys and locks. All manufactured by the same company. It's a very common ... *fetish-based* company, in fact."

I don't even have the brain fortitude to dish out another lie, or to claim ignorance, or to say a thing in my defense.

Maybe I don't want to.

Kevin is standing over me with authority, quite literally holding my freedom in the palm of his big, strong hand.

Isn't this my fantasy? Isn't this happening right in front of my face?

Isn't this type of situation exactly what I have been dreaming about for countless nights?

"Is this a key to such a toy?" he asks simply. "And not to your apartment door?"

I swallow. I feel both shame and excitement with my every heartbeat. "Yes."

"So you were lying earlier?"

"Yes."

"Yes what?"

I stammer, "Y-Yes, sir."

"So the question is," Kevin finishes, "what toy are you hiding, to which this little key goes?"

He had the key hidden in a drawer in that desk.

He found it the night before. He's known about it all day long. He even knew about it this morning, hence his calling out to me through the bathroom door, practically taunting me.

He knew exactly what I was rummaging for.

What if this is the real reason he canceled his important dinner plans tonight?

What if he's been longing to dominate me as much as I've been dreaming of it myself?

And so, as if addressing a god at the top of a grand mountaintop, I keep my small eyes on his, high above me, and I answer him: "It's a key for my Cock-Lock 3000."

For the first time in history, my words cause a reaction on Mr. Kevin Kingston's face.

The corner of his lips pull up the width of a single strand of hair. There's a knowing glint in his eyes, which harden ever slightly.

That look in his eyes sends my heart galloping down a long-abandoned road of terrifying ecstasy, a road I thought overgrown with neglect.

"The 3000 models," Kevin says suddenly, "are particularly unforgiving."

Wait.

Is he *actually* familiar with them, or is he just toying with me even further?

"Are you wearing it now?"

I can barely breathe with my heart racing this fast. "Yes, sir, I am."

He enjoys an agonizing handful of seconds just staring at me after that reply.

What is he mulling over in that mind of his?

"Okay," he finally says, still pinching that key between his big fingers, held hostage as much as my dick is. "Take off your pants."

I gape.

He has to be fucking kidding me.

"A-Are you serious?" I manage.

Kevin says nothing. He only stands over me, his eyes sitting heavily on my face like two round chunks of iron, dark and demanding and personal.

I answer my own question: *Yes, he's serious.*

When I lift myself from the couch, it feels like someone else operates my body.

Then I can't seem to do anything else.

Kevin stares down at me, and I stare back.

I can't do this.

Then he repeats: "Take off your pants."

And suddenly I can.

My fingers—which are somehow slathered in butter, apparently—fumble for my belt. *I'm not Garret,* I tell myself. *He's not my boss. We're just two dudes in a hotel room who met off of a website.*

My pants drop heavily to the floor.

Despite my assuming he'd be staring at the suspicious bulge in my underwear, Kevin's eyes remain on mine instead.

There is something incomparably special about that. How he's so focused on me, and it's intense, yet somehow not overtly sexual.

He says: "Take off your shirt."

My fingers leap to the buttons at once.

The shirt slides off me like an inconsequential fold of fabric, falling to the floor.

My black boxer-briefs feel particularly tight.

And the air in the room feels suddenly cold.

I fight an instinct to cover up my crotch, even though Kevin isn't looking at it at all. He's staring right into my eyes and hasn't glanced away once.

I point at my underwear. "Do you … want me to take … to take off my …?"

"No. How long have you been wearing it?" he asks crisply, cutting me off.

"Since the morning before we left."

"Friday morning, then." He nods appraisingly. "I imagine you feel some *pressure* down there."

"Yes, sir."

"Any abrasions? Soreness? Tenderness?"

"No, surprisingly." I cross my arms, then drop them to my sides, unsure what to do with them. *Am I being interviewed here or something?* "It has been more or less comfortable to wear, with the … exception of … when I get …" My face flushes.

"Hard?" he lends helpfully.

I take a jagged breath, then nod quickly.

"Are you hard now?"

"No, I'm not," I answer dutifully.

"Do you want to be?"

I blink. How does he do that? How does he get right into my head with the perfect questions?

Without a doubt, he knows every answer to every question he asks me.

Even the ones to which I gave him lies at first.

I can't comfortably answer him, and he can clearly tell, because he takes two steps toward me and puts himself right in front of my face. He towers over me by a foot, so maybe it's more accurate to say he's got my face in front of his broad chest now.

My whole world is that crisp white shirt of his and his bold blue tie.

I had pulled that tie out of his suitcase, folded it up nicely, and placed it in a drawer with the rest of his delicates. *I wonder what underwear he's got on underneath those tight, fitted slacks.*

"I told you I need more than promises," Kevin reminds me. "I need you focused this week."

"Yes, sir. You did, sir."

"And in order to accomplish that, I'm going to need to motivate you."

Okay, my dick is starting to swell. Well, at least it's feebly trying to. "M-Motivate—?"

"Kneel."

I drop to my knees instantly.

As if he wasn't towering over me enough.

Now he's really as tall as a mountain. My face is in front of his crotch, right where a lowly, horny guy like me belongs.

I've never felt so small and powerless before.

And loved it so much.

When Kevin looks down on me, his eyes are dark and smoldering. I feel like a shallow pool of boiling water beneath him, waiting for his big feet to walk all over me and cause a careless splash.

"You're kneeling in front of a man."

"I am," I agree. *God, his voice is so clean and crisp as a bell.*

"And I've got a dick that's free as free can be."

"Yes, you do," I agree as well.

"I can get hard if I want. I can fuck if I want." *Oh my God, I've never heard Kevin talk dirty like this.* "I can masturbate if I want. I can itch it. I can wrap my hand around it and feel it swell in my palm." He tilts his head. "Do you miss that kind of freedom, Mr. Haines? Do you miss the feel of your own dick swelling in your grip as you stroke it?"

Fucking hell, he's killing me.

"You're squirming right now," he notes. "I see it in your desperate eyes."

Jesus fuck holy hell shit fuck.

"Go ahead." Kevin nods at me with force. "Put your face in it."

I blink, then stare ahead at his crotch.

"Put your face in it," he repeats.

I close my eyes, then press my face against his crotch.

My happy nose finds itself nuzzled somewhere between his dick and his thigh.

He's hard. He's really fucking hard.

"*Mmph*," is all I can manage to say.

"Do you like having your face buried there?"

"*Mmph*," I confirm, breathing him in.

He is all man.

Refreshingly clean despite our long day.

So warm, and thrumming with sexual tension.

"You want out of your cage, Mr. Haines?"

"*Mm-hmm*."

"How badly, Mr. Haines?"

"*Mmph, mmm, mph*."

A finger touches under my chin, then lifts it gently. I open my eyes to find Kevin's dark-as-coal ones bearing down on mine.

"Then you'd better be focused and impress me the rest of our time here," he informs me, his tone practically polite, "because if you do, then I might consider letting you out."

My eyes flash as I stare at him in shock.

"I hope you understand what I'm saying." He lifts the key up, still pinched between his fingers, and with a little wiggle, makes the key dance. "I'm hanging on to this until the conference is over."

Oh my God.

He closes his fingers around the key, and it's so like the cage itself closing around my cock, sealing it away, gone, poof.

And with a sudden hand placed on the back of my head, he guides my face right back into his warm, throbbing crotch—like returning home.

"*Mmmmmph* ..." is my intelligent response.

And in a cage within my tight underwear, my dick stiffens to capacity, pushing against its metal confines with frustration. I can feel my pulse in my damned balls. The pressure is building up so much, I can't even fathom how I'm going to sleep tonight without any relief. Is it even physically possible for a man in his mid-twenties to have a wet dream?

"Your dick is mine," says Mr. Kevin Kingston from high atop his mountain.

Oh, I believe it.

[5]

*Thursday night is a calm night, the streets cleared of
their usual bar-hopping noise and ambiance. The
atmosphere is strangely serene, even the rumble and
whizzing of traffic seemingly nonexistent.
It's just as well, because Dean is a nervous wreck,
standing at his closet, unable to pick out a shirt.*

DEAN

I need a shirt that says: "I'm approachable, I'm
cool, and I'm an open book."

Instead, every shirt I try on says: "I'm a liar."

This sucks.

This was a bad idea.

Why am I full of nothing but bad ideas lately?
Between the double-date dilemma, which almost
destroyed two of my best friends' love lives, and now
having some ridiculous game night with my ex-
girlfriend from college, her surprise son, and her evil
older sister who hates me, I'm on a clear path of self-
destruction.

Maybe my gut feeling was telling me *not* to have them all over.

Why else am I terrified?

"Want to do a little parade for me?"

I sigh at the sound of Sam's voice. "Babe, I'm having a clothing crisis here."

Sam comes up behind me and wraps his big arms around my waist. "Well, past experience tells me that you look good wearing nothing but a pair of tiny briefs and a bowtie, so ..."

"I have to tell you something."

Sam's hands rub up and down my stomach, now and then a finger going high enough to graze one of my nipples. "I know."

I freeze. "You know?"

"I've given it a lot of thought. The news of her being in town. Your reaction. Some things you've said to me before that I've never had a chance to place until all the puzzle pieces fell together."

I stare at him, uncomprehending.

Sam's big, warm hands slide up to my chest, where he squeezes me against his body. "She's a high school girlfriend."

I'm seriously somewhat astonished. Did *he* have some kind of magical gut feeling? "You ... gathered that fact ... from just ...?"

"You've got to quit underestimating me." He spins me around, kisses me on the lips, then eyes me. "I read people for a living. It's all that business people do: read each other all damned day long. Handshakes and stiff smiles and anxious glances. It's like a game of poker. Even the shine of your shoes can tell so much." He kisses me again. "You told me you dated girls before."

Now I'm super astonished. "I did?"

"Yep. When we first started dating, years ago, way before the wedding. I remember you told me that, and I thought to myself, 'Hmm, I've never dated a bisexual guy before.' I mean, you didn't *identify* as bi, but ... well, it was my thought, nonetheless."

"Wow."

"You don't remember telling me at all?"

"Not in the slightest."

"So your ex-girlfriend is coming over with her son and her sister for a little game night. What's there to be worried about? You can all catch up on old times. And I'll hold back on the PDA."

I am two breaths away from hysterical laughter at my husband's insane mind-reading abilities. "Do you still call it PDA when it's in your own home?"

"You have nothing to worry about tonight." He kisses me again. Then again. Then he puts a hand on my chest, plays at my nipple, then slides his smooth palm down my abs to the bulge in my tight black underwear, where he starts to massage. "Mmm, babe, but you have *plenty* to worry about right now."

He's got such a way with me. "Is that so?"

"Yep. Because assuming I have to behave with you tonight, I'd better get my horniness all out of my system *right now*."

I bite my lip to suppress a grin. "How much time

do we have?"

"Fifteen, maybe twenty. Depends, of course, on the punctuality of your friend."

"That means we have well over an hour."

"That's plenty." Sam drops to his knees, tugs down my underwear to free my throbbing dick, then shoves my back against the wall.

CAYSEN

I stand in the lobby with my now-crumpled-up program, watching most of the crowd dissipate in little clusters of chatter and laughter. Some stick behind, like myself, probably waiting on various cast members to come out of the dressing room.

I lean against a pillar by the front glass doors and listen to an older couple discussing how great the lead performer was. "And the top of act 2 when he discovered about his—?" "Oh, yes, yes, what a moment! So telling. And then he glanced down at the letter—" "Such exquisite storytelling. So much can be said with just a single look."

Blah, blah, blah. They're talking about the lead actor, some boring, bland guy flown in from LA. All I've heard since the show ended is praise for that fucking boring, bland lead guy. The dude had odd lips, a weird nose, and his hair was annoyingly perfect. I wanted to punch him in the face from the moment he stepped foot onto the stage.

But Wade … Wade stole the show in my eyes. He played the role of Jeffrey, who was a cousin who came into town with bad news. He also had a drinking problem. Wade was so fascinating, I kept my eyes on him every scene he was in.

I wonder if this is basically what love is.

Being stolen away by someone.

I check the time on my phone, then glance the other way out the window. Something about the dissipating crowd reminds me of one of the first plays I saw of Wade's in college. I didn't get half the story, too busy literally just staring at Wade in his cute overalls-and-straw-hat costume (it was some country farmer something-or-other play). But I remember afterwards when all his friends came rushing toward him in the lobby after he emerged from the dressing rooms all cleaned up, and I watched from the back somewhere, feeling so far away from his world, feeling like he was untouchable.

And now he's my boyfriend.

It all happened so fast.

Life is so fucked up and sadistic sometimes. It always lifts you up with a good time, but you don't get to fully enjoy that good time because you're all too familiar with what comes next: *the deep, dark plummet of shit hitting the fan.*

Life is just a long series of waiting for shit to happen.

Maybe that's what tonight's play was about.

Meanwhile, the old couple still lingers. "Oh, I know, I just *loved* when the lead had to handle the news from—Oh, what's his name?"

"What's *whose* name?"

"The guy, Gerald! The drunk cousin!"

I push away from the pillar, and as I walk past them, I say, "Wade Lockhart, that's his name, and he's the best goddamned thing about the show."

The old couple stare back at me, affronted.

It doesn't matter. I'm already gone.

I push through the side door no one's supposed to go through—one of those "authorized members of the company only" doors—and listen to the loud banter of the cast and crew laughing and chatting and calling out at each other from dressing room to dressing room. Crew people dressed in all black with headsets on are scurrying around, not one of them seeming to pay me mind. Each dressing room I pass, the door is wide open, regardless of whether it's women or men or both in them. *Theatre people are so shameless.*

When I finally make it to his dressing room— where he and three other actors are crammed—I find him in front of a mirror, shirtless, and cleaning up. "I totally went up on a line," he's in the middle of telling someone, "but no one seemed to notice. It was just that my *cue* line was messed up—*Thanks, Jerry!*—and it threw me off. But hey, you just gotta go with it, no matter what happens."

"The show must go on, I suppose!" agrees the man next to him cheerily.

Wait a second.

That's—

Wade's eyes catch mine. "Caysen! Hey, you!" He gives me an enthusiastic wave from his mirror.

His two visitors turn around.

It's his mom and his dad.

I step into the dressing room. "Hey, there," I greet him. Then I give a reserved nod to his parents one at a time. "Mr. Lockhart. Mrs. Lockhart."

His mother, a woman with a smooth spread of tawny, highlighted hair cropped at the chin, returns my nod with a stiff one of her own. His father's lips spread into a flattened smile, and he nods back while folding his arms.

It's not that his parents hate me or anything. They just happened to have been around during our college days. And maybe I got Wade into trouble a few times, and might've been halfway responsible for him almost failing a class.

Wade sets down his wipes, all covered in the tans and beiges and creams of his makeup he just wiped off, and comes right up to me. For a second, he isn't sure whether to kiss me or just hug me, a flicker of insecurity in his eyes. Then, as if mentally saying, "*Fuck it*," he throws his arms over my shoulders and plants a kiss right on my lips.

He peers into my eyes. "I'm so glad you came. Tonight was a billion times better than last night's dress. The dress rehearsal was a *disaster*."

My hands have instinctively gone around his waist,

my fingers grazing the waistband of his underwear, which peeks out of the top of his jeans. His skin is sweaty (the heat of being under those stage lights is no fucking joke), which is why he's still shirtless, I'm fairly certain. That, and he probably loves flaunting all his hard work on his body.

But with his parents staring at us in confusion across the dressing room, I can't exactly hold a sweaty, shirtless Wade in the same way I would if we were alone. So I just give him a little buddy-slap on the back, then nod toward his makeup table and say, "Don't let me interrupt you, bud."

Wade's smile is strained, but he says, "So glad you came," again, and rushes back to his table to resume cleaning up.

His parents are still staring at me.

Belatedly, I realize that Wade just kissed me on the lips in front of them.

They're probably … wondering things.

And so, with all my best skills of diplomacy at hand, I announce to them: "We're a thing, now."

Wade was wiping down his face in the mirror. My words cause him to freeze at once. He glances at me through the reflection, wide-eyed.

His mother seems to be politely waiting for me to also announce that I'm joking.

His father's thick blunt eyebrows pull together, like he didn't understand what I said, or is trying to interpret "we're a thing, now" in some other way that *doesn't* mean "I fuck your son, now".

Wade lets out a sudden nervous titter, turns to his parents, and apologetically says, "It's a bit new. That's why I, uh … h-haven't …" He swallows. "… told you guys yet."

"Ah," is all his mother says, then smiles.

Her smile is so tight, the poor woman is giving herself a facelift.

The two other actors in the room have finished up, and after a hurried, "See ya tomorrow, Wade," they make their exit, but not after eyeing me with wonder, likely not having known of my existence until tonight.

Bless them.

"Do you have an … opening night cast party thing?" asks Mr. Lockhart after clearing his throat.

"They're throwing a cast party at Tim's tomorrow, but I'm not going to go to it, I don't think. Cays and I have a wedding on Sunday."

His mother hears the words wrong. "What??"

I take another step into the dressing room and lean against the makeup counter next to Wade. "A couple I knew from college are getting married," I clarify helpfully—and calmly. "I was invited and am gonna take Wade as my plus-one."

She calms down in an instant, but her face still looks like she shat a brick in her lace panties. "Yes, I see. A wedding. That sounds … nice."

"Is there an open bar?" asks his dad, a severe look in his eyes. "Wade and alcohol—"

"Dad, I know, ugh," mutters Wade. "I'm a bad drunk. I get stupid. I know."

I chuckle wryly at that. "I'm a worse drunk. Last time I drank, we fought, and I needed Sam to half-carry me home and put me to bed."

His parents eye me worriedly.

This is going so well.

Wade, ever so desperate to change the subject, shoves everything into his makeup kit with a bang. "Cays, I'm going to have dinner with my parents." He quickly pulls on a shirt, then faces me. "You're totally welcome to join us if you want. It's up to you."

Wade has a history of inviting me to dinners with his parents last minute.

I turn to his mom. "Are you okay with it?"

She seems to be yanked out of a daze. "Sorry? What? Who?"

I was determined a second ago to antagonize Wade's loving, overprotective, awful parents. But in an instant, some alien version of Caysen Ryan who is a totally mature adult has taken over.

I want to make peace. I want them to respect me.

My words are gentle and patient. "Are you two okay if I join you for dinner? I'll pay," I add. "The treat will be mine. But I'll totally understand if you guys would rather have time alone with your son."

Wade's parents glance at each other.

All I ever want to do is be around Wade. Yet here I am, surrendering to his parents and putting them first. It isn't lost on me that they rarely—*and I mean rarely*—ever attend Wade's performances. His mom is probably still half-convinced that her son might drop his life here in the city and pursue a law degree after all. It's been her lifelong dream for him.

Wade's mother faces me and, to my surprise, stiffly replies: "You're welcome to join us."

Her tone is somewhat taciturn, but her effort in trying to keep her mind open is appreciated, and I return her words with a warm smile of my own.

Sometimes, the only way to win is slowly.

An hour later, the four of us are at a favorite Asian-fusion restaurant of Wade's in the heart of downtown, plates and bowls of flavored meats, soups, dumplings, and rice set between us. The ice that sat heavily in his parents' chests at the theater has all thawed out, and suddenly we're four laughing, chatting fools, drunk on happiness after Wade's opening night.

And when his parents excuse themselves to go to the bathroom, Wade and I turn to each other. The same thing seems to be sparkling in both our eyes. "You did great tonight," I tell him sincerely.

"You're doing great right now," he says back, inspiring us both to smile, then we sneak a long, labored kiss before his parents return.

GARRET

I am in the hotel room on my knees again.

I know. That's basically how every scene in a porno starts.

But this time, Kevin's on the couch with his big, wide, socked feet propped up on the ottoman.

It's in front of that ottoman that I'm kneeling.

With my tired hands massaging those feet.

Kevin's feet.

This may look like slave labor, torture, or just plain cruelty, but for a guy like me, it's heaven.

How does he manage to keep himself smelling good, even at the end of a long and tiring day, after walking for hours around this gigantic complex, from conference to conference? It's like there isn't a foul thing that emits from this big, clean man. I wonder if he even farts.

"You were still distracted today, Mr. Haines."

My nose is almost buried in his feet when I lift my chin up to gaze at Kevin. It's like staring down a valley of his legs in those black slim-fit slacks, up to the mountain of his chest, broad shoulders, and coal eyes.

"In the conference at noon that took place in the Horizon ballroom," Kevin goes on strictly, "I recall specifically a groan of pleasure you let out when I reached over and grabbed my toy."

That's literally what he did. We were sitting in the far back corner, and no one was in our row. Without any warning or expression on his face, he slipped a hand into my lap and cupped my crotch.

I couldn't help it. A gasp escaped my lips. My cock flexed in reaction.

And then he gave my metal-caged cock and balls a slow, firm, unforgiving squeeze.

The groan slipped out.

One head turned.

But by the time the eyes landed on us, his hand was back in his own lap like nothing happened, and I was left there with this stupid expression on my face, and a desperate dick that was now, once again, outgrowing its metal clothes.

"I'm sorry, sir."

"Not to mention the *other* incident in the Palm Springs room," Kevin goes on. "The one involving my other toy: your tight, muscled ass."

All the air is escaping my lungs at the sound of his stern, crisp voice. He's referring to a moment earlier when we were gathered for a conference, there was standing room only, and once again he had me at the back of the room.

And his hand slowly crept onto my ass.

I noticed, and all my muscles froze up, horny with anticipation.

Then he slid his hand down the back of my pants with expert stealth. His fingers closed around my whole right ass cheek, for a second allowing me to marvel at the size of his hands.

Just the anticipation had me hard—well, as hard as I could get in my cage.

And then he squeezed it.

My dick responded instantly with a flex.

I was literally a squeeze toy. Like the kind you squish their bottom half, and the top half bulges out and squeaks. Whenever he'd squeeze my butt, my dick flexed. Squeeze, flex. Squeeze, flex.

Each squeeze made me melt with pleasure.

Each flex made my dick ache with pressure.

Every time reminded me of the prison my dick was trapped in, reminded me of who was able to free me from that prison, and reminded me of who *owned* me without question.

Mr. Kevin Kingston. My boss. My everything.

"Yes, I remember, sir," I tell him. "I'm sorry. I shouldn't have—"

Squeaked.

Yes. Just like a squeak toy.

On his sixth mighty squeeze of my ass in the middle of that sea of businessmen, I let out the biggest, groaniest, moaniest squeak that the porn industry has ever heard. It was a whimper of agony and delight and longing, all braided together in one magnificent, squeaky squeak.

Several heads turned. Some eyes caught mine, then wandered off. Some faces looked perplexed, searching for the noise.

I clamped shut my lips, wide-eyed.

Kevin, as usual, remained perfectly stoic and did not react. His hand also remained right where it was: cupping my thick ass cheek in my pants and daring me to make another sound.

I didn't dare.

"I don't believe that toys are supposed to make noise," remarks Kevin Kingston. "Especially in the middle of a conference."

"I'm so sorry, sir."

Kevin wiggles his left foot. "You're neglecting my left."

"Yes, sir." I switch my hands to his left foot, giving it the same loving I've been giving his right.

I've gone from loathing my predicament to loving it. Kevin turned a tragedy of a lost key into fulfilling a sexual fantasy I didn't know I had. My heart has been racing all day long. The joy is so overwhelming and endless that I've barely eaten a thing all day.

Seriously, a state of prolonged horniness is the greatest appetite suppressant. I don't know why someone isn't marketing this right now.

My sexuality has never been centered around orgasms. It's based on predicaments I get myself caught in, or guys who take charge over me, or hot and horrible situations in which I'm nothing but an object for another man's amusement.

This is the perfect combination of all of that.

I knew all along that Kevin Kingston would satisfy these dreams of mine—but only when they were just dreams. I never, ever thought it would be something I'd know in real life, something as real as the meaty feet my hands and thumbs are digging into, as real as the chastity device my aching cock keeps pushing against every time I flex it, as real as the dark, demanding eyes that stare down at me from the couch, dominant and knowing.

I want this to last forever.

I want to be Kevin's boy, and Kevin's toy.

I want to belong to nothing and no one else.

He draws out a small, delicate chain necklace he's wearing that was hidden under his dress shirt. A small charm hangs from it.

Then I do a double-take.

It's no charm. It's the key.

"After today's events, do you believe that you deserve to get this back?" he asks lightly, playing with that chained key between his fingers.

I stare at that key.

I stare at it long, and I stare at it hard.

I don't ever want to be free. I don't ever want to be let out of this. I want to stay in this room with you and be your toy forever.

To those dark and brooding eyes of my boss, I answer: "No, sir."

The corner of his mouth curls with approval.

DEAN

Sam and I are a sweaty mess when we're done.

That means we need to take the fastest showers in the world, get dressed in ten seconds, and look presentable for our guests: Izzie, her sister Janie, and her son Derrick.

Sex was exactly what I needed to calm down.

I'm so fucking okay with anything now.

"Ready?" asks Sam as we stand at the door.

I give him a kiss on the lips, say, "Let's wreck this game night," then pull open the door to greet our opponents.

Sorry, I mean guests.

Izzie is a vision in a cute blue top, hip-hugging jeans, and heels, her big spread of hair beautiful and lush. Her sister is a comically stark contrast: a tall, gaunt vision of the Ghost of Christmas Future, her eyes steely and her face unbecoming, but who's judging? She hates me anyway.

"Hey, Dean!" exclaims Izzie, who has clearly coached herself into acting overly cheery seconds before arriving on our doorstep. "Hi, you must be Sam," she then greets my husband. "My, you're so handsome!"

Sam laughs. "And you're stunning. Come in, all of you!"

When the ladies step inside, they reveal a boy who patiently stood behind them like a ghost.

A boy substantially taller than I expected.

Perhaps six or seven, if I had to guess. Brown eyes. Messy, short spiky hair, richly brunette. He's got a button nose and a quiet, sensitive demeanor, which is all too apparent when he peers up at me.

But there's something guarded and dark in his eyes, a close relative of fear, like caution.

I wonder what his mother said to him before they knocked on our door.

"Hey there, buddy," I greet him. "You must be Derrick. Your mom's told me so much about you."

That's a lie.

We're already starting with lies and I only just met the kid. *Way to start on the wrong foot, Dean.*

After a coaxing (and slightly annoyed) gesture from Izzie, Derrick steps inside and nods at me, but still doesn't say anything.

I smile and chuckle at the ladies. "He's a shy one."

Izzie returns my chuckle with an apologetic shrug. "He's like this around new people. He'll warm up."

Janie just stares at me, aloof and weird.

Tonight won't be a disaster. Everything will be great. Nothing to worry about at all.

"Let's get settled in, then!" I tell them, guiding everyone inside. "I'll show you all around. We've got snacks, drinks ... *and tons of games*," I add with a wiggle of my eyebrows at Derrick.

Derrick cracks an infinitesimal smile. Then it fades as quickly as it came.

Well, that's a start.

After a quick tour and a serving of drinks (I'm the only one who takes a glass of wine; everyone else goes for water and tea, the bastards), the five of us settle in our living room with the TV on, and we chat lightly about everything that's transpired in the past ten years.

Okay, I'll be first to admit, most of what Izzie tells me goes in one ear and out the other. I'm too distracted with the weird way Janie keeps looking at me, as if constantly suspecting me of murder, and Sam keeps making weird excuses to try and pull me into the kitchen, but I ignore every one of them, determined to keep the flow of conversation going. The last thing I need is to step aside with Sam so he can whisper and gossip about them with me. Can't he wait until they're gone and we can talk behind their backs like decent human beings?

"Who's ready for a game?" I offer during a lull in the conversation when everyone is just listlessly staring at the TV screen, which I haven't once even looked at. "We can start a round of *Pictionary*, if you guys like that. That one's fun, though I *suck* at drawing." I look over at Derrick. "Can you draw?"

He looks at me, pouting, and just shrugs.

I lean toward Izzie. "He's warming up."

"Is that what you call this?" she asks, returning my sarcasm.

I clap my hands, unintentionally startling Janie out of a daze. "Alright, we'll play teams!" I then announce. "But we'll mix it up! Your sister and Sam will be on one team. Me, you, and Derrick will be on the other."

Sam peers anxiously across the room at Janie, who returns just as awkward a stare.

An easel is set up, the deck of suggestion cards are on the table between us, and thus begins the arduous task of trying to have fun together.

First up: I have a most lovely and awkward experience of drawing the word *THRONE*. Izzie and Derrick stared at my weird doodle on the easel while I urgently gestured at them. "Thimble ...?" suggests Izzie, confused. "Thumb? Garden gnome? Rocket? Ooh, is it a rocket? It's definitely a rocket!"

Derrick only sits there in silence, clearly not in the mood to play.

Time's up.

"Throne," I mumble miserably.

"You should've just drawn a chair and put a king or queen's crown on top," criticizes Janie with a huff.

I laugh. "Well, if you were on my team …"

Izzie sighs at her sister. "Janie, hush."

That comment earns Izzie a severe look from her sister, who does not appreciate being hushed.

Goodness, this is a disaster.

Sam and Janie, however, make the perfect team. Who knew? Every single time it's their turn, they guess each other's drawings in a matter of seconds. With each win, the two of them strangely warm up to one another, laughing now and then at our expense when we do horribly.

And every round, we do horribly.

"Is it a cake?" I call out from the couch when it's Izzie's turn to draw. "A button? A pie? A piece of pie? A donut?" I sigh. "Is it edible at all?"

"Time!" shouts out Janie, proud of herself. Sam high-fives her.

Izzie sighs dejectedly. "It was a *plate*." Then she erases the board.

I purse my lips in frustration.

But the night comes to a head when it's little Derrick's turn to draw.

He plucks his card from the deck, peers at it for all of a half of a second, then walks up to the easel.

The moment he starts drawing, Ms. Competitive Janie flips over the little hourglass, starting his minute or two of time.

Izzie and I, desperate for a single point in this miserable game, immediately start shouting out the most random answers.

"Star!" cries Izzie.

"Flower! Biscuit! Butthole!" I cry out.

"Popcorn!—*goodness, Dean, your language, a child's present*—Icicle! Christmas!"

"Uvula! Tetanus!—*look, I'm just trying to get us ahead here, alright? We're behind by almost six points*—Rabies! Rotavirus! Malaria!"

"Xylophone! Pony! Married couple!"

"Lovers! Bed! Lovers in a bed with …" I stop. My lips form a frown of thought as I stare at his picture longer and longer.

Izzie hasn't stopped. "Tadpole! Circle! Sun! Egg! Embryo! Fat! Belly! Pregnant! … B-Baby …"

And now it's Izzie who's drawn quiet.

Sam and Janie are also staring at Derrick's big drawing, too, which is looking a lot more like a long, complex sentence than it does a single word.

No one even notices the time run out.

Derrick steps away from the easel, then slowly faces us. "Birthday."

I blink, still staring at his picture. "Uh …"

Sam is equally as bewildered. "Is that …?"

"Sweetheart …" starts Izzie, her eyes looking as if they might fall out of her face. "There was … probably a much, much simpler way you could've drawn that word. Like, a cake. Candles. A birthday party hat, one of the pointy ones."

What we're all staring at, by the way, is a drawing of a man and woman in bed, then a sperm wiggling its way into an egg, and then a baby.

I stare at Derrick. "That's quite a drawing for a little lad of your age. Uh ..." I let out a nervous titter. "How old are you, again? I missed it the first time."

"I never said it a first time," answers Derrick, "because my mommy told me not to."

"*Derrick ...*" hisses Izzie.

I squint at him, confused. "Uh, come again?"

"I'm nine."

"Oh." I let out another titter while Sam stares at me hard, like he's pieced something together that I'm still too stupidly oblivious to see. "Well, that explains it. Though, you're kinda short for your age. I'd have taken you for seven."

"I was born a month and a half early," retorts Derrick dutifully, his voice monotone and simple.

Izzie shuts her eyes and slaps a hand to them.

I glance between them, unsure what's going on. I come to my own conclusion. "Hey, it's fine," I assure them both, then laugh. "When I was nine, hell, I knew what ... what *sex* was. I knew the whole process. I could give a book report on it."

"Dean ..." murmurs my husband.

"Sperm and egg and baby and ..." I laugh yet again, despite Sam's imploring looks and Janie's weird ones and Izzie's face-covering. "It's all good, really. Anything goes in this house! Hah! It's a unique way to draw 'birthday', sure, but hey, *Pictionary* has no rules about that, right? No one's hurt!"

The room is deathly silent.

I am clearly missing something.

Like, *whoosh*, over my head.

I glance over at Derrick, wondering if a look at him might reveal what the hell's going on between all the adults in the room.

Then my eyes fall on the easel again.

And his drawing.

Of the process of ... sex.

Something crawls up my neck, something that isn't actually there, something cold.

It's like sweat dragging down your back, but in reverse. Icy and certain. Like Death's bony touch.

Then my eyes meet Derrick's.

Nine-year-old Derrick.

Nine years ...

Nine years ago ...

Nine years ago, Isabel was my girlfriend.

That cold sensation creeps up my neck further.

Oh my God.

"*I'm so, so sorry*," whispers Izzie through the hand that still covers her face.

Derrick keeps staring back at me, the marker hanging from his fist, his drawing at his back, and his lips forming a strange sort of pout.

That's *my* pout.

"What's …" I start to say, then find my throat clenched up, choking away the rest of my sentence. "W-What's going on here?"

I know what's going on here.

I know exactly what's going on.

"I'm so, *so* sorry," Izzie says again, then drops her hand to reveal a face full of tears. "I'm so sorry. I've been trying to tell you, Dean. I've wanted to tell you. For years and years. But then I learned you're gay, and you're married, and … Derrick, cover your ears." He doesn't. "Dean, I thought, why would I want to r-ruin your life with … with this? And after so long? You wouldn't want to know. Y-You—*Derrick, your ears!*"

"What's going on?" I ask again, and wonder if I even heard anything she just said.

I'm in shock and can't peel my eyes away from Derrick. It's suddenly like a fucking mirror.

That's *my* color hair, without the bleach blond dye.

Those are *my* eyes.

How did I not see this the second this little guy came into my house?

"But then he got older and older," Izzie pushes on through her tears, "and he started asking questions, and we started having f-f-fights because I didn't … I didn't want him to see … to meet … to … or you to … to …"

And now she's full-on sobbing.

Isabel Jacobs, filling my left ear with sobs.

Derrick, filling my eyes with … I don't know.

Sam and Janie have turned to stone in their seats, neither of them even seeming to draw breath.

"We were young," Izzie trudges on. "I was only seventeen. I found out during the summer, after we broke up, after I'd already moved away. Please don't hate me. I'm so sorry."

I can't stop staring at Derrick.

It isn't in my nature to hate. It's in my nature to be understanding.

I set everything aside for my friends. I open my ears rather than my mouth. I try my best to give everyone a sense of comfort, to fill this world with good, to practice what I preach.

I think it's all that emotional discipline that makes me say the completely inane, completely unsatisfying, totally and utterly inadequate words of: "I understand, Izzie. I don't hate you." I say the words to her while still staring at Derrick. Tears sting my eyes. "You … Y-You did nothing wrong."

The room swells with cold, empty silence.

Save for the occasional sniffle from Izzie, who has clearly come undone at every seam.

I can't afford to come undone.

Not right now.

Derrick brings the marker to the still-stunned Sam and quietly offers it to him. "Your turn."

[6]

Saturday night. 8:02 PM.
The sun is still out, but it's saying goodbye.
And so is Garret. To everything.

GARRET

Tomorrow, we return back to our lives.

We'll abandon this grand and luxurious suite and trade it for our apartments and our offices and all the due tedium of boring day-to-day life.

But what happens to ... *us?*

"That was our last seminar," Kevin notes as we leave the ballroom, heading for the dining hall for some formal closing ceremony thing. "Did you get everything on the tablet?"

My answer is a little sullen. "Yes, sir."

Kevin either doesn't notice or doesn't react. "Good," is all he returns.

A vast ballroom downstairs is filled with round tables topped with plates, cutlery, and folded cloth napkins. We sit at one in the center of the room, and we're served a modest Italian meal of bread, pasta, and chicken. I sit there in silence and watch as Kevin makes small talk with whoever these random people are that we're seated with. One of them is a lady who might have been a speaker at a seminar earlier in the week, but I can't quite recall.

You'll have to forgive me. My mind might've been *elsewhere* during that seminar.

The thing is, fantasies are delightful and can be enriching and life-saving when fulfilled. But every fantasy in the world is a double-edged sword that cuts you twice: once *before* the fantasy is realized while you're longing for it in agony, and once *after* it is realized and must then come to an end.

I daresay the second cut stings worse.

How am I expected to go back to my life after this insane, indescribable week?

Kevin reaches into my lap during the dinner. Despite us being in the middle of the room, he seems to choose the perfect time when everyone else is occupied in conversations and no one sees.

He's a man of stealth.

And caution.

And sometimes, absolute brazenness.

His hand slides to my inner thigh.

Despite my glum mood, my dick betrays me, reacting at once to his touch on my sensitive inner thigh. My lips part automatically as his fingers graze delicately over my crotch, cupping my cage, balls, and easily-excitable dick all at once.

I am pure electricity and chemistry down there.

One touch of Kevin's hand, and my mind is desperately flooded by every single dirty thought imaginable.

Then his hand slides out of my lap as slyly as it had slid in, and I'm left sitting there with my heart beating three times as fast as it was ten seconds ago, and my dick vainly trying to fully harden.

I would say Kevin is a total asshole for doing that to me, but I guess that's the cruel trick of these kinds of relationships: pain is pleasure is pain.

It's impossible at times to separate the two.

The dinner concludes sooner than expected, rounds of applause and farewells and last greetings are made, and suddenly Kevin and I are strolling up to the door of our suite.

For the last time.

He doesn't seem too playful at first when the pair of us go to our respective places in the room—desk and couch—to transfer our notes and organize things from this final day. Neither of us even take off any of our clothes, despite him having made me get completely naked (except for the cock cage, of course) last night, and then down to my underwear the night before.

When we're finished with all our work, Kevin simply says, "I'm going to take a shower. I suggest packing your things ahead of time, since it'll be an early morning departure tomorrow."

By the time I glance up at him, he's already disappeared into the bedroom. A drawer opens, a drawer shuts, and then the bathroom door closes with a soft *thump*.

But he left the outer bedroom door open.

Is there a reason for that? Is it an invitation? Is his mind cooking up one last evil night of torment and teasing and horniness and—?

Oh, right, he wanted me to pack my things. My shit is in there. *Ugh.*

I set his tablet and laptop on the dresser near his stuff, then pull my suitcase out of the closet and start tossing my clothes into it. Whatever crap I've left in the bathroom, I'll just have to grab when it's my turn to shower.

After packing everything, I fetch myself a tall glass of water, then stand by the windows of the main room and stare out at the city, like some tall resentful king poring over his subjects.

A king who can't even jerk his own dick off.

And hasn't had any relief for over a week.

And is trying to stave off his tears and not cry like a bitch right now.

I hear the water shut off. Then, a surprising ten seconds later, the bathroom opens. "Garret," comes his voice from the bedroom door.

I turn.

Kevin stands there in the doorway, dripping wet, and naked except for one thing.

His shiny black-and-white compression shorts.

The ones I stuffed my face into the night we arrived and I unpacked his *delicates*.

It's like Jock-Con all over again, except the magnificent football player has stripped off all his gear—his pads, his shoulders, his chest, his jersey, his pants, his cleats, everything—and revealing just his skintight compression shorts.

My eyes flick up from his tight thighs and his crotch, grazing over his man bod that's dusted with the perfect amount of hair, his broad chest, and up to his strong neck.

I was wrong. He's wearing something else.

The key to my cock.

Around his neck.

On a tiny, evil chain.

"I believe you deserve a reward for your hard work this week," Kevin tells me.

I feel so weak suddenly. I have to set my glass of water down on the end table of the couch, then just stare at Kevin, unresponsive.

I have an urge to run up to him and drop to my knees, desperate to have my face in those shorts again, except this time with him *wearing* them.

I have another urge to scream and shout and demand for that key he's got around his neck.

But mostly, all I feel is sad.

"I said I believe you deserve a reward for your hard work this week," he repeats, a touch stiffer.

"I don't know if I'm enjoying this anymore," I blurt out at once.

His face is one of little expression, so when his eyes narrow in the slightest, its impact is strong.

"I …" My throat is trying to shut itself as I speak. My mouth is dry. *Why did I just say that?* "I just … I think I needed to … to be honest. I needed to be blunt and honest and … a-and blunt."

He nods at me. "That's what I want."

I lift my eyebrows, worried.

"Honesty," he clarifies. "That's all I want from you, Garret." He crosses his arms and leans against the doorframe. "Go ahead. Speak your mind."

That pose he's suddenly in does absolutely nothing to help me focus on my point.

There's a whole couch and a small table and maybe eight or so steps between us. This room is so fucking big.

"I've been enjoying this," I start out. "I have. A lot. So much that it makes me—"

"Sick in your gut?" he offers.

"Yes!" I exclaim. "And a part of me loves it. But this … this *other* part of me is starting to wear thin. It's becoming *actual* torture now. It's like I've … reached my actual limit or something."

Kevin gives me his full attention. His eyes are so keen, I feel like he heard even beyond the words that came out of my mouth. Even now that I've stopped talking, he's still got this pensive, curious look on his face that makes me want to keep on, pouring out my whole life story right here.

Kevin breaks the silence by taking a breath, and then he pushes away from the doorframe and approaches me. "Thank you for speaking up."

"You're welcome." The words come out, then I wrinkle up my face. *You're welcome? Really?*

Kevin stops by the end of the couch closest to my side and sits on its arm. He peers at me sharply. "I was keeping this key to prolong your pleasure. Once the pleasure's gone, the game is over."

The game is over …? "What?"

"I'm not interested in hurting you. Or torturing you. Or causing you unhappiness."

"Y-You're not causing me unhappiness," I say quickly, backpedaling. "I'm very happy."

Kevin tilts his head. "Well, we can't play this both ways, Garret. You can't tell me you're happy, but also not enjoying this anymore. Which is it? Are you happy? Or no longer enjoying this?"

"I'm … I-I'm both."

Kevin exercises a great deal of patience with me. It's evident in the fact that there is no sign of annoyance for my fickleness, or my inability to describe how I feel.

He gives me the time I need to sort this out.

He waits for me and he listens.

He doesn't push me. He just speaks and asks questions and clarifies my confusion.

I've never felt safer expressing myself before.

"Let's try something," Kevin decides. "Instead of focusing so much on this key around my neck, or that cage around your cock, or the fact that it's Saturday and we're about to return home in the morning …"

"That's *all* I'm thinking about," I admit.

Kevin's eyes stay on mine, sincere, unmoved with humor or lightness. He's so serious and sharp and focused all the time. "How about you simply tell me what you want right now?"

I stare at Kevin, unsure if this is another part of the game.

Seeing my indecision, he adds, "Suppose for this moment we're not playing a game of cocks and cages. We're just Kevin and Garret. We're not even boss and employee. Just Kevin. Just Garret." He gives me one curt nod. "What do you want?"

My eyes drift down his body in thought, then land on his crotch in those smooth, shiny, tight black shorts. It isn't even sexual, my absentminded staring. I'm genuinely asking myself the question: *What do I want?*

Then the answer hits me. "I want a hug."

Kevin's eyebrows pinch together.

Remember that big stoic his-face-never-shows-reactions thing?

Only the soft sound of our breathing fills the space between us. That, and a tiny grumble of hunger in my stomach.

Bad timing, I know, but I could really go for a fat fucking burrito right about now.

As if gently drawn out of the shadows and into a bright room, Kevin squints at me as he rises from the arm of the big, long couch, a look of mild intrigue in his dark eyes.

I stand right in place, staring back.

Kevin takes three very slow steps toward me.

With each step, my head inclines upward some more, keeping our gazes locked.

He stops in front of me, looming over my head like a great god who's stepped off Mount Olympus to greet a humble mortal.

You hear that? I went from being a resentful king to being a humble mortal in minutes.

"A hug," he repeats, gazing down at me.

I wince. "It's stupid. I know. It's—"

"It's not." While this close, his gaze switches from my left eye to my right eye and back again, searching my mind with curiosity.

Slowly, Kevin wraps his arms around my body and gently hugs me against his bare, wet chest. His skin is still warm and damp from his shower. His modest patch of chest hair smells like fresh soap.

As for what happens next, I can't help it.

And I can't explain it.

I break down and cry.

Throughout my whole body. Like a seizure while standing up. All my woes burst out of me.

Kevin's hold on me tightens. His hand gently and slowly starts to rub up and down my back.

I stop crying abruptly. My throat squeezes shut and I stare dully at the smooth flesh of his upper shoulder in silence.

"Feel better?" asks Kevin ever so quietly.

I find myself smiling. Then I murmur, "You know, I kinda figured I'd get my relief when I finally came." I chuckle. "Not from *crying*."

Kevin keeps slowly rubbing my back. "There's no shame in crying."

"I just feel so ... so *embarrassed*."

"Why?"

"Because I'm crying in front of my boss."

"And that embarrasses you?"

Every question of his sounds infinitely deeper than it seems at first. Suddenly I wonder if I ought to rethink everything I know about crying and shame and authority. *Should crying embarrass me? Should I be embarrassed at all?*

The question sounds so philosophical now.

"You're getting a hug," says Kevin in an even voice. "Now that you've gotten what you wanted, is there something else you realize you want?"

I wonder if this is a puzzle.

My sadistic, creative mind assumes that, since he's in charge here, this is really just his way of tricking me into some kind of horny, permanent-cock-cage trap. Now that I've cried, my dirty mind rushes forward like an eager puppy, ready to play again.

But I have Kevin in a unique spot right now. I have to be smarter than my dick.

"Yes," I answer.

"Tell me. What else do you want?"

With my arms wrapped around Kevin's warm, wet body, I deliver my answer to his chest. "I want you to kiss me."

His breath touches my ear when he turns his face ever so slightly. Even with my head pressed to his chest, I feel his intense stare upon the top of my head like the rays of a dark sun.

Maybe he isn't the kissing type, I worry. *What if I ask him for something he isn't willing to give? What if I ask for too much? What if…*

He gently pulls away, his every move sensual and careful, and stares into my eyes.

I swallow and look up at his, nervous, waiting.

Then he touches the bottom of my chin with a finger and pulls it up, bringing it higher, almost too high, exposing my neck.

His hand lightly moves to my neck, where he takes a peculiarly gentle hold. *Fuck, his hand is so soft.* If someone were to look at us, they'd think he was strangling me one-handed.

But he doesn't squeeze.

He holds me there and brings his mouth right in front of mine, then stops in front of my face as he burns my eyes with his.

"You want me to kiss you?"

His hand on my neck becomes erotic instantly.

Especially when I feel the vibrations of my own voice in his palm as I answer: "Yes."

He stares at me for a long, pensive while.

Then he kisses me.

It feels so good that I instantly want to cry again. His lips are so soft. His kiss is so loving and unlike anything I would have expected from him.

I suddenly can't remember the last time I was kissed at all.

His hand shifts on my neck, his thumb pressed against the underside of my jaw, his other fingers wrapping around the side of my neck, holding me right in place as he kisses me with deep intention.

Even with just a kiss, he manages to make me feel completely owned, completely like an object, completely his.

When the kiss ends, both our eyes open, as if from a dream, and we study each other's faces.

I lick my lips, tasting him. "I …" Again, I feel the vibrations of my own words in his hand. "I … feel really, really good right now."

Kevin's hand slides down my neck and rests at the top of my chest, right on the fat knot of my tie. "Do you feel safe again?" he asks me.

"Yes."

"Do you trust me?"

"Yes, I do."

Kevin lets go of me, then slowly proceeds to undo my tie and remove my dress shirt. He gently takes my hand and leads me to the bedroom. My heart echoes the *thump-thump-thump* of his heavy footsteps. He guides me to the bed, then gestures at it without a word. I sit on the bed at first, unsure what he's expecting me to do. Again without speaking, Kevin places a hand on my chest, and after a firm look at my face, he pushes me down, pressing my backside to the bed, my legs dangling over the edge. I stare up at the ceiling as Kevin's hand slides down my chest, down my abs, and stops abruptly at my crotch.

I hear my pants unzip.

My heart jumps.

He slips a hand in through the fly. With a tug, the front of my underwear is yanked down from within, and after a few maneuvers, he manages to pull my cocked cage through the fly of my pants.

The moment I think about peering down my body to see what he's doing, his hand slaps to my chest and presses me right back down.

I stay right where I am, my heart thrashing in his palm, my eyes glued to the hotel ceiling.

I hear a tiny clinking of metal.

Tap, tap, tap.

And then at once, my cock and balls are freed.

Oh. My. God.

The skin drinks in cool and rejuvenating air, breathing for the first time in over a damned week. Impatiently, my freed cock starts to harden at once, desperate for the liberation it was just given.

"*Oh, man ...*" I moan, shocked. "*That's intense.*"

Kevin's voice comes from down between my legs where I don't have a hope of looking. "I said earlier that you deserve a reward for your work this week. I meant it."

He could punish me, torment me, or pleasure me. Any of it would feel like a reward right now. I am in pure ecstasy just from being freed from that fucking evil toy.

"Your reward is my warm, wet mouth," he so politely informs me, "and the pleasure it gives you, wherever I put it."

"*Oh, God,*" I intelligently respond.

"Your reward is *not*, however, getting to come. That happens when *I* decide. Do you understand?"

"P-Perfectly, sir." *Are we back to doing the sir thing? Is that alright? I'm pretty much done with crying and being emotional now.* "Oh, man …"

When Kevin's mouth wraps around my stiff, throbbing, desperate dick, I know nothing at all.

His hand keeps pressing against my chest, as if to squeeze all the air from my lungs and quiet my racing heart. His mouth is both warm and cool as it swallows every inch I have.

Heaven itself knows no bliss like this.

No orgasm can match the *feeling* right now of being utterly at the mercy of another man's mouth.

His torso pins my legs down. His one big hand pins my chest and upper body down.

I am all his. Tied down without ropes. *Pinned.*

It shouldn't be a surprise that in just forty-three seconds, I'm already so close, I could burst with no warning. I mean, we're talking about over a week of pent-up man juice inside me.

Sure, I've gone longer than this before. I've done weird shit. I've been kinky. I've been owned.

But I struggle to remember a single time in my life that I've felt this complete all around: sexually, emotionally, *and* mentally.

Everything aligns with Kevin Kingston.

Everything is perfect.

His mouth comes off my dick. Then he grips it with his other hand and, now slickened from top to bottom by his wet mouth, he jerks me off.

There's some kind of magic about a hand job immediately following a blow job that makes my whole body six billion times more sensitive.

I squirm beneath him and claw at the sheets.

My toes curl automatically.

"*Kevin, Kevin, Kevin ...*" I moan.

He doesn't stop or slow down.

"Are you ready to come?"

"Y-Yes," I moan out. Then: "No. No, not yet. I want this to last forever. *Mmph, God ...*"

"You're going to come when I tell you to. It doesn't matter if you're ready for it or not."

"*Mmph, please ...*"

"I know you don't want this to end. That's why you've kept this going so long. You're afraid once it ends, it'll be gone for good."

I feel a pinch of fear at his words—and a pinch of surprise at the truth in them. "*Y-Yes ...*"

"But a real player, he isn't afraid of the finish line, is he? Every game has a goal."

I'm not sure, but I answer anyway. "*No ...*"

"He goes out and he plays the game, no matter what. He does what he's told. He doesn't let down his team. *He plays the game.*"

"*Yes, he does, you're right. Yes, God ...*"

"Are you close?"

"*I'm so, so, so close ...*"

He lets go of my dick, lets go of my chest, and rises to his feet.

I look up at him, catching my breath.

"On your knees."

I sit up at once, then slide right off the side of the bed and drop to my knees in front of Kevin.

My face is right at his crotch. He stares down at me with iron-hard authority.

"Sir," I murmur, my wet boner throbbing, my breathing coming in and rushing out with urgency.

"Jerk yourself off," he orders, "but don't come."

Keeping my eyes glued to his, far above me, up the mountain of man that is Kevin, I bring my hand to my hard, slick cock and stroke it.

With a touch of sweetness, Kevin places a hand on the back of my head, then slowly pulls my face into the tight, shiny black crotch of his athletic compression shorts.

My eyes shut drunkenly as I breathe him in, clean and manly and powerful.

Clean.

Manly.

Powerful.

I feel his big fat dick against my cheek through the shiny, tight material, like his dick is hugging me.

Oh my God, he's so hard.

"Feel safe with your face buried in there?"

"*Mph*," I answer.

"Is that where you belong, Garret? With your face buried in a better man's crotch?"

"*Mmm-hmm,*" I moan, nearly in tears again, tears of overwhelming joy and belongingness.

"Are you gonna be my boy whenever I want? Even after we leave this hotel?"

"*Mm-hmmph.*"

"After we're home?"

"*Mph.*"

"After we're back in the routine of our lives?"

"*Mmmph, mmph, mmm.*"

"All good things come to an end," he says to the top of my buried head, "but who says the world ever runs out of good things?"

I start to shiver.

My balls are tight.

His dick pressed against my face flexes, strong and big and mighty as a man's dick can be.

My mouth opens onto his crotch automatically, and I breathe deeply and without abandon against his swollen dick through the shiny material.

My lips press against it.

It's as if I'm desperate to maneuver the big thing into my mouth.

I've never wanted anyone so badly, so obsessively, so desperately.

Something is about to become very inevitable.

And soon.

"Are you trying to get it in your mouth?" he asks, and though his tone is sincere, the words seem taunting to my ears. "My big fat dick?"

I can't even begin to describe.

What Kevin's dirty talk.

Is doing to me.

"You want it in your mouth, Garret?"

"*Mmph.*"

"You do?"

"*Mm-hmmph.*"

"How badly?"

"*Mmmmmph.*"

A hand curls into my hair, grips it tightly, and pulls my head back. His other hand hooks into his shorts, then tugs them down.

His hard dick flips out and smacks my cheek.

I peer up at Kevin from the foot of the mountain.

A set of hard, hungry eyes stare back down.

Then he moves his hips, putting the head of his dick right at my lips. I open my mouth, desperate.

And with a simple thrust forward, he dives into my mouth.

Kevin Kingston is so big, he covers my whole tongue. My mouth is stretched overwhelmingly wide. With thrust after thrust, Kevin mercilessly fucks my warm, wet, stretched-open mouth.

My eyes drink in his thick, squared hips as they dance, little muscles flexing and moving in his thighs. With one hand I keep jerking myself, but slowly now, not daring to creep too close to the edge and disobey Kevin's strict order to not come.

My other hand, however, has no instruction at all.

While he fucks my face, it slides up his leg, now and then catching on his smooth hairs.

"Go ahead," he grunts from high above. "Keep going, Garret. Keep that hand going."

It slides up to his thigh, now sliding over the shiny, smooth material of his black compression shorts.

"Keep going."

His voice is becoming strained.

He seems to be enjoying this as much as I am.

My hand creeps up his thick thigh, which flexes with his every thrust at my face. My mouth and jaw know no relief as they stay stretched for his big dick to glide in and out over my tongue.

"My ass, Garret," he commands. "Grab a big, big handful of my ass. Do it. It's yours."

Do it?

It's yours?

When I'm given that permission, my hand reaches around him and slaps a big, great handful of his ass, just as ordered. *Fuck me, it feels exactly the way I have always dreamed.* It's dimpled and tight on the sides, yet perfectly plump and soft enough to squeeze. He just yanked his underwear down from the front, so the shiny material still covers his ass, and I'm forced in my blindness to imagine its prestige.

Then his dick slides right out of my mouth, and he starts jerking himself right before my face. "I'm going to come all over you," he tells me.

My lips are wet, my mouth is sore, my eyes are glued to Kevin high above me. "I want you to come all over me, sir. Please, sir. Please do it."

I never thought I'd hear myself say those words.

To anyone. Ever.

In fact, this may be the very first *and* last time you ever hear those words come out of Garret Haines' lips.

"Get ready," he tells me, then grips my hair even tighter and pulls my head back.

And then he releases all over my face.

When it first hits my cheek, I shut my eyes and open my mouth. Wave after wave of warm, perfect Kevin juice covers my cheeks, lips, and chin.

His grip on my hair relaxes.

I open my eyes and peer up at him.

He says: "I'm not done with you."

The next instant, Kevin grips me, lifts me right up like a sack of nothing, and tosses me onto the bed. He crawls onto the bed next to me, pins me down with one hand on my chest, and grabs my dick with the other.

As he jerks me off, he stares down into my eyes, a vicious excitement radiating from his own.

"*S-Sir* …" I breathe, overwhelmed.

"Not until I say," he reminds me.

I'm already right on the edge. I'm squirming. My toes are curling.

"*S-S-Sir* …" I try again, whimpering.

"Not until I say."

My hands claw into the bed. I'm breathing hot and hard. His juice is all over my face and in my beard. I don't dare look away from his handsome, commanding face as it hovers over mine.

Then I gasp his name: "*Kevin*."

And he says it at last: "Come for me, Garret."

Not a second later, I shoot, my mouth wide open to release a great, unrelenting war cry.

Relief, at long last.

Kevin doesn't relent as he jerks my now-sensitive dick with constant speed.

I come so hard, and I come so fucking much.

It's absolutely endless.

Shot after shot bursts from me and lands across my abs, up my chest, even hitting my face.

I've never had an orgasm last this long.

Nor rocket out of me with such vigor.

The aftershocks of my orgasm ache in my gut, in my balls, even in my stomach.

When his hand stops moving, so do I. My mouth hangs open and my eyes go droopy. Kevin's hand stays on my wet, sticky dick, like he still owns it, as he stares down at me with a dark fascination. My lungs empty into the air above me over and over as my heart slows.

I could live right here in this place forever.

When Kevin lets go of my dick and starts to rub my chest gently, I barely notice, still stuck somewhere between a dream and the reality of what just happened.

My sex-drunk eyes slowly open to find Kevin's right in front of my face.

I smile, feeling silly. "Well played, Kevin."

Surprisingly, he returns half a smile of his own, and throws a peck of humor right back at me: "Good game, Garret."

[7]

*Sunday morning flows in like an unnoticed flood in the
basement, quiet and calm and seemingly small, then
heavier and more alarming as time passes.
And that is precisely what Dean Addicks-Pine feels in
his troubled heart: alarm.*

DEAN

I've been staring at the same mug of coffee for probably twenty minutes. Maybe it's even been an hour by now. I don't even know.

"Babe, you've been staring at that same mug of coffee for an hour now."

Well, that answers it.

I turn to look at Sam in his boxers, who's come down to the kitchen after finishing up something in his upstairs office. "Morning, babe."

He smiles at me. "You alright?"

I shrug for an answer.

Sam comes up to the counter and slips an arm around my waist, hugging me to his side.

After a bit, I say, "Everything's so weird now."

"Hmm. Did last night not go so well?"

I peer down at the mug again, from which I've not taken a single sip.

It's been a very long weekend since that bizarre and revealing game night on Thursday.

Izzie and I took all of Friday to think things over on our own. She took that time to explain to Derrick the truth—namely, that I'm his father. Sometime in the evening on Friday, she called me up, we both had a few things to share, and then we agreed to meet up at a park on Saturday—yesterday.

Our time at the park was at first, to say the very least, awkward as all hell. Derrick didn't know what to say to me any more than he did during game night. Izzie was timid and strange. (Janie had stayed behind at the hotel.) I kept trying to keep the mood light and receptive as we strolled through the park, but my heart was tangled with the worry that everything was simply unfixable between us.

Then Derrick revealed to me that he had an interest in magic, sorcery, and people with special powers.

"Ooh, is that so?" I asked him. We were under the shade of a particularly large tree. "I happen to have a special power."

Derrick peered at me dubiously, but it was certain to me that I had caught his full attention and curiosity.

"I get these *feelings* in my belly," I told him. "In my heart sometimes, too. They're like premonitions. I call them my gut feelings. They warn me of things."

"Is it a magical power?" he asked me, excited.

"I think it is. It must be. Once, it even saved my friends' lives, as well as my own."

Derrick's eyes flashed with wonder. In an instant, he was a different person. "Can you teach me? I want a special power. I want to use magic."

Izzie was watching us with her own version of wonder on her face, half-hiding a smile, seated on a bench nearby.

I crouched by Derrick and smiled up into his face. "Well, as it turns out, you're my son. And if we are to believe that my power is real, then that *must* mean that a part of that magic lives in you, too."

I put my hand on his belly. He flinched and peered down where my hand lay.

"Right here," I told him, inspired. "You ever feel anything strange, right here? A fear that comes out of nowhere? A fear that brings you great pause?"

Derrick considered my question, looking almost afraid as he did. Then, ever so slowly, he began to nod.

I smiled. "Then the magic's in you, too." I leaned into him and raised my eyebrows with warning. "*Listen to it, Derrick.*"

To that, he gave me an assured nod, and said, "I will. I promise."

The rest of the day was bliss. Izzie, Derrick, and I continued through the park chatting about life, dreams, plans ... and a lot about "magic".

I had a good gut feeling all day in the park.

Last night was a little different.

Izzie and I met again, alone, at a quiet coffee shop near her hotel. Over two cups of mediocre coffee, the curious pair of us had a *real* heart-to-heart, without Derrick present. I told her my feelings. She then shared her own. We both cried. We also had a few laughs. And then it hit me like a sudden left hook.

I really am a father now.

And I've *been* a father, unknowingly, for a little over nine years.

"Last night went alright, I guess," I finally answer Sam, fidgeting with my mug, spinning it around on the counter, bit by bit. "Izzie was always a sweetheart. I know it in my heart that she didn't mean to hurt me. Or to leave me out of my son's—" *Fuck, it still feels so strange to say that.* "… my son's life."

"Well, you're not left out now," Sam points out. "Look at it this way, babe: you really only missed the annoying diaper-changing bits."

I smile at Sam, knowing he means well in his attempt to cheer me up. I give him a peck on the lips, then say, "They headed back this morning."

Sam nods knowingly. "Don't worry. They'll visit again. Or we could go out and visit them, y'know. I've got so many airline miles, babe, I could send you off to visit them twenty times a month if you wanted."

I snort at that.

"Listen to me." My husband faces me importantly and takes my hands, pulling them away from the mug. "You've been telling me for months now—*years*—that something's been missing from your life."

I bow my head, listening.

"You kept trying to start businesses over and over. You kept taking it upon yourself to host our events here at the house, despite me having guys who can deal with all that."

"Ugh, but the *choices* they make for the catering, seriously, ugh ..." I start.

Sam continues on. "You care for all your friends— Garret, Wade, and Caysen—as if they're your blood brothers. As if they're your true family."

"I don't have any actual blood brothers," I mutter thoughtfully.

"You've been desperate to fill a hole in your heart, a hole I've known of for years." Sam then squeezes my hands, peering into my face. "Maybe *this* is that thing you've been looking for."

I stare at him in wonder. *A son ... my son ...*

"She wants you to be a part of his life," Sam reminds me. "It's why she came all this way. She may even still be in love with you, in some ways. Dean, there is space in all our hearts for more love. Your son wants you in his life, too. He wants a father. He's the one who badgered Izzie into revealing who you are."

I look at Sam. My heart's so full, it might spill over somehow, just like this mug of cold-ass coffee, if I dare to fidget with it anymore. "You really think so?"

"I know so." He places a hand on my cheek. "I think you've been destined to be a dad. You're built for it—caring, selfless, devoted. I'm the luckiest man to have snatched you up and put a ring on that finger."

That particular combination of words makes me smile without reservation. I throw my arms around Sam and pull him in for a tight, squeezing hug.

His big hand rubs my back in slow, soothing circles as we embrace, comforting me.

"You're wrong," I say over his shoulder.

Sam's hand stops on my back. "Hmm?"

"It's *me* who's the lucky one."

He chuckles dryly, then pats me gently. "A good husband knows when to refrain from arguing with his stubborn, adoring lover. So he will let you be the lucky one. For now."

I turn my face and give his ear a little nip. "A good husband also knows when his boy's feeling frisky on a Sunday morning." I pull away and eye him. "And his boy is feeling *very* frisky."

Sam grins. He sweeps me right off my feet and carries me off to the stairs laughingly.

And a sad, unnecessary mug of cold coffee remains right where it is on the kitchen counter, its curved ceramic body catching the glare from the light of the morning sun.

GARRET

I'm cuddled in my boss's arms in a king size bed of an executive suite with bright and beaming morning sunlight pouring over our naked bodies.

In other words: Who the fuck am I?

"What's going to happen when we get home?" I ask, my voice filling the room.

We've both been awake for the past hour. We only got three and a half hours of sleep last night, maybe less. See, after I finally came, I jumped in the shower, and then Kevin surprisingly joined me. We both got horny again, and a bunch of strange occurrences happened in our room. Some involved us naked, some involved us fully clothed ...

And some involved us just relaxing on the couch together, cuddled, and watching TV. Around two in the morning, it started to rain, and we shut off the TV and watched the raindrops tapping down the floor-to-ceiling windows of the suite, neither of us talking.

When we decided to finally go to sleep, Kevin surprised me by taking my hand and inviting me into his big, king-size bed.

I guess I should have expected it or something, but it was surprising nonetheless.

Of course, we didn't end up sleeping yet. We stayed up another hour and a half talking about our lives, our interests, our childhoods, our strange and "yet totally natural" sexual interests ...

I've never felt so fucking normal before. *What a weird thought to have while in your boss's arms.*

Kevin considers my question. "When we get home, I'll be your boss, and you'll be my model employee. Just as we were."

I frown. "Where's the fun in that?"

"We have roles we must play in the office. We keep it professional. We keep our focus on our jobs. Of course …" He shrugs. "… *outside* of the office is a whole different thing."

"Do we have to be so abstract about it all?" I don't mean to sound like I'm complaining, but I can't help my mildly annoyed tone of voice. "Does it always have to be such a … such a *game?*"

"What do you mean?"

I sit up and face him on the bed. "Can't we just be boyfriends? You be mine, I be yours?"

Kevin studies my face for a while. Even in the morning, going on little to no sleep, the man looks perfectly put together, crisp and aware.

"Well, do you *want* to be boyfriends?" he asks.

I hesitate, hearing his question out loud.

He goes on. "Do you want to date?" He lifts his eyebrows, genuinely curious. "And do you want me to bring you flowers on our anniversaries? Do you want us to be like a normal, conventional couple?"

I hear him. And I realize the truth. "No."

"No?"

My eyes are steady and as focused as his. "No, I don't. I …" *Wow, my mind is exploding.* "I … don't want that at all."

"Are you sure?"

I stare down at the plain, endless white sheets in which we've been tangled throughout the night.

His questions have suddenly made me feel so wise. My whole life suddenly feels like a big pile of notes, much like the ones I've been taking all week, and they're spread out before my eyes in clear, uncomplicated detail.

"I was never a conventional boyfriend guy," I admit suddenly. "I don't exactly hook-up, but I'm hard-pressed to find a guy who'll give me love … *and* an experience. Every boyfriend I've ever had doesn't get it. They just get frustrated with me … or bored." Then I lift my eyes to him. "But I like you, Kevin. I like you a lot. And sometimes, I want the best of both worlds. I want a guy I can be … *creative* with. But also a guy who'll cuddle me the way you did, holding me while we sleep. I want a boyfriend who's not really a boyfriend. I …" My own contradicting words make me laugh. "I guess I want to have my cake and eat it, too."

Kevin gives my answer a lot of thought. Then he squints at me and tilts his head. "I've always thought that was such a ridiculous saying: 'Can't have your cake and eat it, too.' Who in their right mind would get a cake and *not* want to eat it?"

I laugh at that. Kevin just gives me this odd, amused half-smile, still appearing so strong and stoic, even with the tiniest smile on his face.

When my laughter dies away, I shrug. "So let's eat the fucking cake."

Kevin nods. "Let's eat the fucking cake."

The rest of the morning is as easy as cake itself for us. We get room service for breakfast. Apparently the whole "pack your things early" thing was just him being bossy, because our flight isn't nearly as early as he'd made me fear it was. Before heading off to the airport, I give the big room one last look over, sigh wistfully, then follow Kevin through the door.

When we're finally on the plane, I discreetly tell him: "I packed the, um … *toy* … away in my things. I think we've had enough of it for a while."

"A while, perhaps," agrees Kevin.

Then I lean in closer and whisper, "*Keep the key. You know … just in case I'm bad.*"

To that, Kevin smirks knowingly, and nods.

WADE

The midafternoon Sunday wedding reception is a mess and a half of drunken idiots, loud partying, and ear-blasting music. Caysen and I sit at a table, alone, in a sea of tables that once held calm, cake-eating people.

Now, it's surrounded by partying, horny men and women as well as about a hundred screaming fools I don't remember seeing at the wedding itself—*which was totally gorgeous and amazing, by the way.*

Well, mostly. "Marriage is so fucking … *weird*," I mumble, watching some guy do a funky dance nearby.

Caysen chuckles and shakes his head tiredly. "This *wedding* is so fucking weird."

"Oh, the drag queen bridesmaids were kinda cool, actually," I point out. "I kept staring at their makeup and being like … *damn* that's gotta take hours."

"I'm sure it does," Caysen agrees with a grunt.

I glance over at him. He looks like such a stud in his fitted suit and bowtie. I could tear all his clothes off right now and do him on the table in front of the world. The reception is so wild, I doubt anyone would notice.

But something else washes over me.

A feeling that's more sensitive, more wholesome, softer and more durable than lust.

I don't know what it is exactly, but it makes me ask: "Do you see us lasting?"

Caysen looks at me, his eyes wide and his brows yanked together. "Where the hell did that come from?"

"We're at a wedding, you dummy," I point out unnecessarily. "Where do you think it came from?"

"Fair enough. But what are you getting at? Are you asking if I see us getting married someday? Going through all this shit? Picking out tuxes and color schemes and cake flavors and fighting over the seating arrangements?"

Our arms are nuzzled up against one another's. There's no one else at our table, yet we can't seem to pull apart from each other.

I give him a coy little smirk. "Yes, actually. That's exactly what I'm asking."

Caysen gives me exactly five seconds of hard staring before he says: "You fuckin' bet I do."

His blunt answer makes me laugh. The laugh makes me throw an arm around him, and suddenly our lips meet in the middle. One sensitive, gentle kiss turns into a firmer one.

Then our hands get involved, and nothing can pull us apart.

Until I pull us apart. "But do you mean it?"

Caysen huffs at me with impatience. "Dude, is this some kind of test? I'm trying to fuck your face with my mouth."

"It's just ..." I wonder if this is the real issue that has been on my mind for weeks now. "I ... have a hard time separating ... the Caysen I've *known* ... from the Caysen I *know*."

Somewhere behind us, a conga line has started, and a bunch of loud, near-naked guys (who are clearly too sweaty for their tuxes now) are using the line as an excuse to grind on one another. Some dude is asleep atop a nearby table, hugging a flowery centerpiece and snoring. A woman near him is eating a single piece of cake, alone, and staring wide-eyed at the festivities.

And at our secluded little table in the middle of that mess, Caysen's eyes search mine for a while after my declaration. From the way he hesitates to respond, I worry that I've either hurt him or angered him.

So I try, through the noise of this loud outdoor pavilion, to clarify: "Cays, it's something that everyone knows. You like to hook up with your clients."

Maybe I was too blunt. Caysen's face pinches with pain. "Are you suggesting I'd cheat on you?"

"My heart says you wouldn't. My mind says it doesn't make sense for you to ... unless after you get enough of a taste of this *fantasy* we're living ... you get ..." I shift in my seat. "... bored."

Two glasses shatter in the distance. Some woman screams, then laughs. We ignore it. "Bored?"

"Like, what if I don't live up to your fantasies of me?" I suggest. "What if we get ... 'comfortable' with each other, like Dean and Sam did their first year of marriage? What if we stop having sex?"

"I'll stop having sex with you when I'm dead."

"And then after we're comfortable," I go on, still worrying like crazy, "what if you suddenly ... get this hot new client at the gym ... and your thoughts stray away from *us*, and suddenly—"

"What if you get cast in some show," Caysen throws back, cutting me off, "where you play the lover of some super *adorable* guy, and between rehearsals and performances, a bunch of *real* feelings are sparked between you two?"

I sputter, taken aback by the tables being spun around on me. "I ... w-wait a sec, I—"

"And how about all those rehearsals when you gotta kiss another dude who isn't me?—a really, really *hot* guy? You would be literally kissing another guy's mouth five times a week, ten times a week, and with every rehearsed kiss, it would get more and more passionate, more and more real."

"I'd never do that," I swear at once.

"You'll *have* to," Caysen states right back at me, firm as stone. "You're an actor. It'll be asked of you many times. You can't avoid romantic roles your whole acting career, Wade. Or sexy costars. Or hot crew guys dressed in all black helping you quick-change backstage. It's gonna happen, just as likely as it is that I'll get hot clients."

I slump back in my seat, defeated.

Caysen gets right back in my face, and his tone turns soft. "My point isn't that this is hopeless. My point is that we're gonna have to trust each other. I'm just ..." He lets out one breath of a laugh. "I'm just ... gonna have to work on some of my jealousy issues. You know I have them. I'm possessive and I got eyes on every dude who looks your way. There's been thirty of them at this damned wedding alone."

I gawk, then glance left and right. "Where are these mystery admirers you keep insisting I have?"

Caysen shakes his head at me while a smile spreads over his face. "You're so fucking cute and unaware sometimes."

I bring my uncertain gaze back to his. "So your answer is ... I need to just trust you?"

He gives me a slow nod at first. Then his eyes drift down to my chest, a thought brewing in his mind. Reluctantly, he shares the thought: "Whenever I used to ... bring some guy back to my pad ..." He lets out a snort. "I never looked at it this way until now. Maybe never realized it. But ..." He meets my eyes. "Want to know the first thing I always thought when the clothes started coming off?"

I lift my eyebrows, listening. "What?"

He says: "'*When is this gonna end?*' That was always my thought. Then when it was over, I just sat there in the bed, ready for the guy to leave. He would sometimes linger, like he was expecting to stay over, or chat and get all emotional and lovey. I didn't want any of that. I just wanted him gone."

Some guy in a tux stands up on a table nearby, dancing and slowly stripping off his vest. He gets cheered on by a bunch of drunk people around them, their friends, maybe. Another guy hops on the table with him, the two grinding on one another.

Meanwhile, Cays and I are trying to have this deep moment here. "I didn't know," I start to say.

Caysen takes my hand. "I think everyone ... Garret, Dean, even you ... imagine my life one way. As if it's some endless party and my gym is nothing but a muscle buffet."

"I don't!"

"You do. I don't blame you, but you do. And the truth is," he then says, "I have loved you for so long, Wade, and ... I just didn't know where to put all those feelings. I was terrified that revealing them would ruin what we had. Our perfect friendship."

"So you fucked your way through the city to try and get over your feelings for me?" I conclude for him in a syrupy voice, my words dripping with sentiment. "What a sweetheart."

Caysen eyes me. "Are you mocking me?"

I break a smile. "A little."

The stripping guy on the table near us stumbles and falls off into the crowd, inspiring a lot of loud laughter mixed with screams. Two or three chairs are knocked over. The music gets louder.

Caysen brings his face closer to mine and puts an arm around me, as if to shield me from the noise and the commotion.

"I love you, Wade. That isn't something I'm just saying to win your heart. I want you to know the real me, all of me, even the uglier parts, because then you'll know I'm in this for as long as you'll have me." He smirks. "And you'll know I mean it when I say: *yes, I see us lasting.*"

I bite my lip. This isn't exactly the ideal, sweet Sunday wedding setting that would befit this kind of a conversation, but my eyes still fill up with tears at the sweet sound of Caysen's words.

And to his eyes, I reply: "I do, too."

I do. What an interesting choice of words.

Then the passionate pair of us kiss deeply at that lonely table in the middle of a sea of tables, the noise of the crazy reception falling right away all around us, and nothing else in the world matters at all.

[EPILOGUE]

Two months later.
A warm, early evening. The sun is setting the distant
city skyline afire as it gives way to night. The summer
is drawing to an end, but this party sure isn't. It's one
of Sam and Dean's big business gala things held at
their townhome. The wine keeps pouring. The hors
d'oeuvres keep coming around. And Caysen observes it
all from the second-floor banister, full of thoughts
about all that's passed this summer.

CAYSEN

I've tuned out the soft murmur of the crowded
townhouse. I've tuned out the ivory-tickling from the
hired pianist downstairs. All that sits with me is a
pensive look on my face, a soreness in my arms from
this morning's tough workout …

And a warm feeling of fullness in my heart.

I've never felt this way before—"in love" or
"content" or "happy" or whatever.

It's not entirely comfortable.

This morning when I woke up by Wade's side in his apartment—which I will now safely confirm *is* like an episode of *Hoarders*, lately—I felt an unexpected pinch of fear. I lay in that bed, peering at Wade's cute, sleeping face, and my heart began to race, and not from excitement.

I suddenly had these other feelings.

Like: what if he's someday gone?

What if some freak accident happens onstage during his next rehearsal? Like a Fresnel light just drops from the grid and lands right on his head?

What if, clumsy and ditzy as he is sometimes, he steps onto the street too early and gets hit by an impatient cab driver?

He meant the world to me when we were just best friends. But now that world is made a lot bigger with just one stupid word: *Boyfriend*.

And all these new possibilities terrify me.

I can't live in a world without Wade Lockhart.

I'm jerked out of my thoughts when a plate of hors d'oeuvres is shoved in front of my face.

I take it, then peer at my generous assailant.

The reveal is less than lovely. "What the hell do you want, Garret?"

Garret shrugs as he leans on the banister next to me. "Thought I'd make a bit of a peace offering. After our … unfortunate *thing* last week."

I smirk suspiciously at him.

It was more like nine days ago when Wade and I decided to go to some interactive bohemian art exhibit, and out of complete freak coincidence, Garret was also there. Garret was with some guy I would later learn is Kevin, his boss, and when they saw us, Garret made this big annoying point of introducing Wade to Kevin—and noting that they dated way back in college. *"Oh, and this is his replacement of me, named Caysen, who is, for some inexplicable reason, Wade's boyfriend now,"* he added, making them all laugh.

It wasn't some super ugly comment. It was just a tad juvenile, in retrospect. But I was having a hard time already trying to act comfortable at that art exhibit, constantly struggling to find intelligent observations to make about all the pretentious art we were seeing, and feeling utterly out of my element. The last thing I needed was Garret's snark to ruin my night and make me feel like some meathead idiot.

So I did what any mature adult would do.

I smacked his self-important drink out of his self-important hand, sending it flying into a nearby exhibit and destroying someone's work of art.

Ten minutes later, I was apologizing to Wade.

Another twelve minutes after that, I bought the ruined piece of art I didn't even want, and was out four hundred bucks.

Another seven minutes later, we were out of the door early and Wade was rubbing my back, telling me I needed to work on my temper.

I know. It's a lifelong flaw. I'll probably need to see a therapist someday and unbury some repressed childhood angst issues or some shit.

But for now, I simply stare at Garret, a plate of fancy finger foods in my grip, and I see a man who can't help his nature any more than I can.

"Sorry for knocking the shit out of that drink in your hand," I force myself to say, curt.

Garret gives me a crushed half-smile. "I think I was feeling uncharacteristically cocky that night with Kevin at my side. It was rude of me, what I said." He shrugs. "The drink was nasty anyway."

I chuckle. "So I did you a favor, then?"

"Yep. It was probably poisoned. Would have given me indigestion all night, which wouldn't have been good, considering Kevin's plan with me to, um ..." He changes the subject. "Anyway, what else are friends for but to knock nasty drinks out of each other's hands?"

I pick up a single cream cheese and prosciutto cocktail bite, consider it for two seconds, then pop the whole thing into my mouth. I chew it with vigor while staring Garret down. Through my mouthful, while still chewing demonstratively, I answer him: "They're for giving advice when it's needed."

Garret pretends to wipe a crumb off his face that flew out of my mouth. "Advice?" He lifts an eyebrow. "You're in need of some?"

I swallow, then stuff in another bite. "Yep."

He wrinkles his face as he watches me chew. I know it's driving him nuts. He's got this OCD thing about watching people eat, or being talked at while someone's eating, or ... I don't even know. I just love antagonizing the fuck out of Garret.

It's a two-way street.

I think we're destined to be frenemies forever.

"So what do you need advice with?" he asks, while trying not to stare at my obnoxious chewing.

I nod. "The one thing we have in common."

Garret screws up his forehead. "Wade?"

I swallow my bite, then smile.

He shrugs. "What's the issue, then? You two seem plenty happy. All he ever talks about when I call him up is how amazing things are. I mean, unless you're paying him to say that."

"Things *are* great. And that's the problem." I face Garret completely. "You and your boss. You guys are, uh … a thing now, right?"

"We try not to define it."

"And you've wanted this … *'undefined thing'* … with him for a long time, right?"

"Yeah."

"So aren't you kinda afraid now? Of losing it? Of doing the wrong thing, fucking up, and ruining this precious thing you've wanted for so long?"

Garret, surprisingly quick on the uptake, nods. "Alright. So you need advice on how to *not* ruin things with Wade. I dated him once, years ago, and you think, despite hating me to the core, that I'm a 'Wade expert' and the only guy in the city who can help you with this specific circumstance. Got it."

"Uh, I didn't say—"

"Here's what you have to do." Garret claps his hands together once, like punctuation. "You need to take Wade on a proper date, but unannounced. Surprise him. Make it somewhere that isn't *too* fancy. He likes pizza, he likes hamburgers, he—"

"I know what he *likes*," I cut him off, annoyed.

"Well, sure, but you've been starving him with your healthy-healthy health food lately and—Look, do you want my advice or not?"

I remain straight-lipped and await the rest of his nuggets of wisdom.

"And once you take him on this date and have fun, you'll bring him back to your place, and have a bottle of Dean's specialty wine ready. It's his favorite."

"I know."

"He'll start to feel weirdly inspired and will—"

"—start to spout off on all the roles he wants to play someday, on his dream to open a theater of his own, produce shows, catch the attention of Broadway and yeah, I know," I finish for him.

"Good. You'll listen to every word he has to say to you. Even when he goes off on tangents that make no sense. *You know how he gets when he starts talking about muses and how 'free' he felt in 'that one acting class in college' …*"

"Hah, oh, I know that, too. If I have to hear about it one more damned time …" I mumble, chuckling.

"You will. And you have to." Garret nods at me. "That's what's going to do it."

"Do what?"

"The trick." He smiles. "To catching him. That's what's going to make him all yours, Caysen. A lot of listening. A bit of sweetness. A bit of sexy-sexy. And nothing else."

With that, Garret plucks a single bite off my plate, crams it into his own mouth, and starts to chew as unbearably as I was.

I stare at him, disgusted by the obnoxious chewing. *Damn, that's what I look like when I do that?*

"I mean, really," he says through his mouthful as crumbs fly everywhere, "what kind of advice did you expect from me?"

"The kind where you don't eat with your mouth full," I mumble back.

Garret ignores the remark. "Wade and you have already been a couple since I've known you," he points out. "I'd daresay it's why none of Wade's relationships ever worked out. No one he dated compared to you. He just didn't know it yet."

"Really?"

"Of course really. He's dense as a rock. Aren't we talking about the same Wade here?" Then, as if an afterthought, Garret adds: "And, of course, if you don't want to take any of my advice … you *could* just jump the gun and do the other thing."

I frown. "Other thing?"

"Yep." Garret pops another one into his mouth. "Drop to a knee in front of him."

I stare at Garret, stunned by that idea.

Adequately pleased with the reaction on my face, he says, "Worked with me and Kevin. Except when I get on my knees, it isn't a *ring* I'm giving him." Garret chuckles at his own joke, then gives a quick wave before hopping down the stairs. I watch him until he fades into the crowd below, feeling an odd new respect for the guy.

And now I'm smiling again.

Because the idea of Wade someday becoming my husband is, in one crazy instant, the greatest notion in the whole fucking world.

DEAN

Sometimes, having a husband is just the worst thing in the world.

You have to constantly worry about what the heck he wants. Or if he's happy. Or if he's hungry.

Kinda like a baby. A big, adult baby.

Thankfully, Sam is no such husband.

He puts all other husbands in the world to shame. Without a doubt, he's the most understanding, kind, thoughtful, compassionate man I've ever known.

When I need time, he gives it.

When I need space, I've got it. Like right now.

And when a fiery nine-year-old dive-bombs into my life, he goes right along with it like it was planned.

"Do I start calling you Dad?" Derrick asks me.

Izzie, who's sitting on the bed poring over an old yearbook of ours that I retrieved from a shelf in the closet, glances our way, wide-eyed.

The three of us escaped the noise of the party for a brief respite in my bedroom upstairs. A lamp is on at my desk where I stand, illuminating a pile of old photos I dumped out of a shoebox. I'm not sure why, but just before the party, we decided to get nostalgic and turned a lesson of how-I-met-your-mother into a big trip down memory lane.

Derrick and Izzie are staying with us while they're in town. I fixed up our guest rooms for them. It was a bit of a pet project I assigned myself the minute they departed from town that first time months ago—a pet project into which I put all my love and attention. I even put on overalls and painted the room his favorite colors (which I had to ask Izzie for), and matched all the bedding and furniture. Sam was more than amused, coming home to a husband spattered in paint and looking as sweaty as I do when I come home from a long session with Caysen at the Weights & Mates gym.

When the room was finished, Sam stood by me and stared into the room in awe. Then he eyed me and said, "You're such a daddy now."

It wasn't the first time I'd heard the joke. Over and over from Caysen, Wade, and Garret, I heard: "Looks like *Sam* isn't the only *daddy* around here anymore!"

My friends took to the news with surprising ease. I guess in their eyes, I was destined to become a father someday. Just like Sam said: it was in my blood.

But now let's snap back to present time. Y'know, the moment when Derrick just asked if he should start calling me Dad now.

I stare at my son. "Uh ..."

Izzie graciously steps in. "Sweetheart, you can call him whatever you feel comfortable with." Her eyes lift to mine encouragingly.

I pick up what she's tossing me. "Of course." I smile at Derrick. "Call me Dean. Call me Dad. Call me Mr. Addicks-Pine. Whatever suits you."

Derrick seems to think it over, then takes a few photos off the desk and studies them, aloof.

Izzie closes the yearbook suddenly. "You know, I was doing some ... *thinking*."

I glance back at her. "Yeah?"

"About what you said."

I blink. As it turns out, I've said many things ever since Izzie crashed back into my life with my surprise-son Derrick. Some things involved the room I'd made for Derrick when he and Izzie visit. Some things were about my eyes being opened. Other things were about teriyaki chicken recipes. Really, she needs to be more specific. "Good thinking? Or bad?"

"Good thinking. Only good thinking."

I lean back on the desk. "What about?"

Derrick picks up a photo and turns to his mother. "Is this you?"

Izzie rises from the bed and crosses the room, bending down to peer at the photo over Derrick's shoulder. "Ooh, I had *bangs*." She looks up at me and winces. "*Yikes*."

I shake my head. "I had frosted tips and guy-liner. Seriously, how'd you *not* know back then?"

"Because you easily pulled off the whole punk, alternative-guy look," she says defensively. "Everyone just ... assumed you were in a band or something."

"All I was missing were the fingerless gloves."

She shrugs. "Well, I guess the ... the *signs* aren't always so *obvious* to someone who ... who grew up without ..." She sighs, frustrated by something.

I come up to her side. "Sorry. I didn't mean to mock you or anything."

"No, no. It's not you. It's ..." She glances at me. "It's actually related to what I was thinking. Before. It's exactly the reason for ... what I'm about to say."

"You mean all this 'good thinking' you've been doing ...?"

Derrick looks over his shoulder at her. "Is this 'good thinking' about that, um ... thing we were talking about on the plane ride here ...?"

Izzie nods. "Yes, sweetheart."

"Oh." He goes back to shuffling through photos.

She puts her hands on our son's shoulders and gives him an anxious rub as she looks up at me. "I don't think Derrick is getting the stimulation his mind needs at his current school. I mean, he's a creative kid. He's got such an ... such an *imagination*."

"Aww. I can tell." I give Derrick a smile, even though his full, undivided, totally-serious attention is on the photos, seeming to pay us no mind at all.

"I want my son to be somewhere where he can bloom. Somewhere that *does* have culture, where he'll grow up and not be *shocked* by the world when he gets out of our town at last. A place that's more ..." She looks around. "Well ... more like here, actually."

I lift my eyebrows in surprise.

Izzie sighs at once. "I know. It ... seems like this is coming out of nowhere. I'm sorry. It's just—"

"Actually," I cut her off politely, "I remember a long time ago when you told me that you always saw yourself as more of a city girl."

She gasps. "You remember that?"

"I remember everything."

Izzie gazes at me. A smile appears in her eyes before it touches her lips.

I nod at her. "So ... you're actually thinking of ... relocating here ...?"

"Well, not *here*-here, exactly. I'm not sure we're ready for the middle of *this* busy city. But maybe a suburb just outside the city. But ... still significantly closer to you than we are now, yes." She smiles a bit. "You did all that work on your guest room for Derrick, he feels like he has his own space here. And he has so much fun whenever we visit." After a short glance at the top of his head, she leans into me and adds, "*I mean, you can't tell, but I swear he does.*"

"I do," agrees Derrick listlessly from below.

"It's not quite a done deal yet," she quickly points out to me. "I mean, I would have to, um ... make a lot of arrangements. My sister and I will probably have a big, dramatic shouting match before she accepts my decision, bless her. My parents, too. But they had to deal with me leaving for college some years back ...

and this isn't so different, is it?" Her eyes turn soft. "Dean, there's simply nothing left in that town for us."

I give her a hug at once. The hug lasts for a while. The only sound I hear is the continual flipping of photos in Derrick's little hands.

Into her ear, full of compassion, I whisper, "*I love this good thinking of yours.*"

Izzie smiles when I pull away to look at her, then nods vigorously. "Me, too."

The door behind us opens, and Sam's bright, handsome, bearded face appears. "Hey!" he greets the three of us cheerily, smiling.

I slip away from Izzie to give my husband a peck on the cheek. "Hey there, babe. Izzie just told me the greatest news ever."

"*It isn't for sure yet!*" she reminds me in a hissed whisper from across the room.

I lean towards Sam. "They might be moving to a suburb right outside the city, close by."

Sam's eyes light up at once, and then he beams his joy at the others. "That's fucking great news!" He winces after a quick glance at Derrick and edits himself. "Sorry. My language. I need to, uh—"

"Oh, don't worry," Izzie assures him sweetly. "It isn't anything he hasn't heard before."

"Fucking right about that," mumbles Derrick.

All three of us stare at the kid, wide-eyed.

He turns around, feeling the silence, and looks at each of us in turn. "Uh, what?"

Izzie bites her lip to stifle a laugh of shock.

"Well, ah, didn't mean to interrupt," mutters Sam, "but the *magician* just arrived, and I heard they—"

Derrick ditches the photos on the desk at once. "I wanna see! I wanna see!" he cries out, then races right past Sam on his way out of the room, ignoring Izzie shouting out at him to wait. Then she sighs, shakes her head, and on her way out after him, says to me, "I hope you're ready, Dean Addicks-Pine, because that boy is a handful."

Sam and I stand at the bedroom door, watching Izzie as she heads toward the stairs after Derrick.

At the top of those stairs, however, Derrick stops and looks back at me. "I think I have magic in me, too. Just like you. I felt it the other day."

I smile, overwhelmed with emotion. "Did you?"

"Yeah. And ..." He nods with resolve. "I want to call you Dad."

Oh my God, I might cry.

But I keep myself together, smile brightly, and say, "That's totally cool with me, Derrick."

The kid doesn't smile (I'm honestly not sure if he is physically capable of it, as serious as he is), but his eyes sure seem to. In a hurry, he rushes down the stairs. Izzie lingers at the top step, her eyes on mine, knowing and full of love, before following him down.

"Oh, man," I breathe when they're off. "That was a moment, right there."

"She is a really sweet person," murmurs Sam, his voice full of dreams and thoughts. "And you're gonna be the best daddy to that kid."

I look at him suddenly, struck. "Is all of this okay with you, babe?"

Sam quirks an eyebrow at me. "You mean now that I'm something like an uncle, or a second dad, and the love of my life just filled that hole in his heart at long last?" The smile he gives me is beaming. "It's a new lease on our life together. And it's beautiful."

Again with that *I-have-the-best-husband* thing. "Have I told you how sexy you look tonight?"

"A few times after we got ready. Then a few more times while we were downstairs schmoozing." He looks me over. "You coming down to see the magic? Or are you ... otherwise occupied up here ...?"

His hand slides down my backside, then comes to rest at the top of my butt. His fingers graze down just a bit more. Then he cups my cheek, giving it a squeeze.

I shoot him a look. "Babe, I think your mouth is saying one thing, and your hands are saying another."

"Yeah?" He pulls my hips against his with force. "What are they saying?"

"Let's shut the door and find out," I suggest.

Sam grins, kicks it shut, and tackles me to the bed with a hearty growl.

WADE

Oh my God there are a thousand billion things to choose from on this buffet table.

But, like, y'know, Caysen's whole "health" kick.

I lick my lips as my eyes eat each and every delectable-looking bite-size dessert and slice of gooey, chocolaty goodness on that table.

I might cry.

I might literally cry.

If I sneak just one little bite, Caysen won't know. That's perfectly acceptable, isn't it?

Finally, I muster up the courage. Using the little metal pincers, I move a cute, dark, swirly chocolate tart-thing onto my plate. My heart races, probably in anticipation of all the sugary badness I'm about to attack it with. *Get ready, nervous system.* I pinch it with my fingers, close my eyes, prepare for heaven, and draw it toward my lips.

"Ah, looks like I came just in time."

I pop open my eyes, the tart frozen between my lips, half an inch away from touching my tongue.

My eyes dart to the source of the voice.

"Haih, Cah-sahn," I say with my mouth staying open, the tart still pinched in my fingers, hovering at my wide-open mouth.

Caysen smirks. "Looks like you were about to put something super delicious in your mouth." He folds his arms. "What stopped you?"

I glare at him as I bring the tart back to my plate, my mouth snapping closed resentfully.

Something about the expression on my face makes Caysen burst out laughing. "Oh, man. You are *so* just torturing yourself at this table, aren't you?"

I smirk bitterly. "Obviously." I set the plate down.

Caysen picks the plate right back up. "Open your mouth, you big dummy."

I blink, stunned.

He picks up the chocolate tart, then brings it to my lips, which I slowly part. When the sweet dark delicacy touches my tongue, I have an orgasm of joy in my gut. My mouth closes around it, and I chew, the rich and sugary taste flooding my tongue and obliterating all of my silly senses.

I peel open my eyes. "*Mmmmmmmm.*"

"Mmm, indeed," teases Caysen, setting down my empty plate and watching me chew. "I think that's the sexiest thing I've seen all week, watching you eat that calorie-filled artery clogger."

Still chewing, I give Caysen a look.

He chuckles, then brings his arms around me and holds me tightly against his chest. "I fucking love you. I fucking love you so much, Wade."

My face pressed to his chest, I swallow my bite. "I love you, too, babe, but you're choking me."

He doesn't let go.

I incline my head slightly, curious. "Is this show of affection coming from somewhere in particular …?"

"Nope." He continues to hold me prisoner within his big strong arms, confined to his chest.

Not that it's too shabby a prison to live in. Caysen and his thick, muscular chest is about the safest place on Earth. I've done the math. It checks out.

"So you're just hugging me because …?"

"Because someday, I'm gonna marry you."

I let out a laugh. Caysen's sense of humor has blossomed over the months we've been together. It's like something inside him—an inner child, an alternate personality, something—has unlocked. He laughs more and is never afraid to smile. He squeezes me randomly, just like this. He kisses me in public.

It's almost gross. But like, in the cute way.

And it's so fucking beautiful.

He doesn't let me out of his arms, but he pulls his head away enough to look down into my eyes. "Wade Lockhart. I'm dead serious."

I smile up into his eyes. "Oh, are you?"

"You bet I am. One day, the world's going to be calling you Wade Ryan. Even your mother, despite the coronary she might have when I pop the news to her that I'm putting a ring on your finger."

"Such a romantic," I sing at him, grinning.

"I'm just stating facts." Then his face turns serious. His eyes harden. "I want you to be mine forever."

Caysen's expression sobers my own. I peer up into his face, his gaze full of resolve. "You're ... serious," I say and realize at once.

"Yes." His gaze jumps back and forth between my eyes. "I've loved you for a very long time, Wade."

"I know. I love you, too, Cays. I always have."

"I'm not interested in anyone else in the whole world. I'm done. You've ruined me for anyone else. I'm done with dating, with looking, with wanting. I'm done with it forever. You're all I want."

I'm genuinely stunned speechless.

"You don't have to say yes ..." he goes on.

I blink. "A-Are you *actually* proposing to me?"

"... but I just want you to know, Wade ..."

"Are you really asking me to be your husband?"

"... that if you have *any* reason to doubt my love for you, *any* at all ..."

"You know damned well I need you to just *say* it, Cays. I can't handle this abstract half-spoken stuff."

He tenderly, yet with firm intention, grips my face with both his hands. His eyes ask the question before his mouth does. "Wade Lockhart," he asks me, "will you someday do me the honor of being my husband?"

With his hands framing my face, my eyebrows are a bit scrunched when I lift them. "Someday?"

"We're young. We have a lot of time to have fun, to explore the world together, to be stupid. We don't have to rush. So yes, someday. Someday. Any day. In a year. In five years. Or tomorrow. Will you marry me?"

The question should freak me out.

It should. It's a very, very big question.

But if Caysen Ryan is the man for me, and I know for a fact that he fills me with more love than I'll ever think I deserve, doesn't that question answer itself?

"Yes."

His eyes flash, as if surprised. "Yes?"

"But ..."

His eyes falter. "B-But ...?"

I bite my lip, then shrug. "Isn't Caysen *Lockhart* a better fit?"

Caysen smirks, then shakes his head. "I don't care what you call us, babe, as long as you're mine, and I'm yours, forever."

And right there by that long table full of forbidden sweets and gourmet delicacies, two boys who were once classmates, who were once roommates, who were once besties, share a sweet and meaningful kiss.

It's our first kiss of forever.

Because I am certain as fuck going to marry this beautiful man someday.

And soon.

GARRET

The secret about the big game is that everyone is a player.

Just some people don't know they are.

"Who was it?" asks Kevin on the phone.

I'm on the upstairs landing, away from the party, so I can hear him clearly. "It was a text from Jeremy, my old friend I told you about," I answer. "He's the one who gave me the Cock-Lock 3000."

"Yes, him. He seems like a generous friend."

"He is," I admit. "He's always been a friend, even if he's sort of ... uninspiring. To be honest, though, I think I may have rubbed off on him or motivated him."

"Hmm. Judging from what you've told me about his latest encounter, I'd say you're right."

I smirk. He's referencing a long text I got a week or two ago from Jeremy in which he detailed a very … *interesting* time he had with two guys he hooked up with off a fetish dating app. Jeremy tried some things that he and I used to do, and what started off as a night like any other quickly turned into some kind of clever, hardcore interrogation scene. Both guys cracked too quickly, using the safe word to get free. Jeremy had thought it was hilarious and texted me about it, saying I would have lasted ten times longer than they did.

"So you think you can last longer than those two wimpy buddies of Jeremy's?" asks Kevin tauntingly through the phone.

I bite my lip, feeling my dick swell in my pants. I am thankfully not confined by any sort of metal cage down there, but … I *might* have another secret toy planted elsewhere.

"Yes, sir," I answer Kevin, feeling daring. "You bet I can."

"Are you sure?"

I hear a click through the phone.

Vibrations explode in my ass.

I fall back against the nearest wall with a gasp. I nearly drop the phone as I bear the full brunt of the toy's merciless vibrating. Both pleasure and pain flood my body, chasing its way through every nerve, to my fingertips, to my toes, to my ears.

Then it stops.

I pant, mouth hanging open, eyes drunk.

"*Fuuuck,*" I breathe into the phone.

An amused snort of laughter from Kevin's nostrils shoots through the phone. "Just remember who owns your cute ass at all hours of the day."

I could be defiant. I could fight back with him, dare him to do that to me again.

But he's gotten smart at my reverse psychology tactics. *You're not gonna top from the bottom so easily with me, Garret*, he warned me once a few weeks ago, right before tying me to a bed and having his way with my desperately hard dick for no less than two hours.

I was so sore the next day.

And deliriously happy.

"I'll never forget," I promise him, smiling darkly.

"I'll be home from this business meeting in about an hour. Come over after the party. I can order us some late-night dinner, if you're still hungry and want to stay at my place again tonight."

His place is big, by the way. Huge. It's located in the uppity part of town, and it's made me completely and utterly forget that grand executive suite, which has got nothing on Kevin's fancy uptown loft.

"I look forward to seeing you, sir," I assure him.

He hears the genuine adoration for him in my little unassuming words—the adoration that transcends any game we play, any role we assume—and he replies, "Me too," in a soft, knowing, sensitive voice.

Then we hang up.

I pocket my phone, a smile pasted over my face, then glance over at the door to the upstairs bedroom, the one with the balcony. A thought percolates.

"You, too?"

I turn toward the voice. It's Dean. "What?"

"You were thinking about escaping onto the roof for a little breather, eh?" teases Dean.

"Man, you must be reading my mind."

Dean pats his heart. "Just call it a gut feeling."

To that, we both laugh, and suddenly we're darting for the balcony door.

In another minute, we're lying side-by-side on the roof of his townhouse, staring up at the stars. I ask him how being a father has changed his life. He points out a star and reminisces on old times. Our hearts are full.

"I knew I'd find you guys here!" cries out a voice.

Dean and I sit up to find Wade and Caysen's heads popped up from the ledge of the roof.

Now it's the four of us lying side-by-side, Dean on one side, and Wade and Caysen cuddled on the other. While the stars twinkle and the city down below honks and squeals and hisses, I share laughter with my friends while Wade animatedly tells us some story about the crazy backstage antics at his latest show. Dean and I nearly scream we're laughing so hard. Caysen, too.

Somewhere during the story, my happy mind runs off, and I find what Kevin said about good times to be true: The game of life never ends. And when you play it with the right people by your side, you always win.

And the world will *never* be short on boys—or toys—to play this beautiful game with.

The end.

ACKNOWLEDGEMENTS

To all the readers who stuck with me throughout the fun process of telling these four boys' stories from Caysen's beginning to Garret's end, I want to sincerely thank you for your heart, your laughter, and your mind. I've greatly appreciated you welcoming my boys into your happily-reading hands these past four novellas.

Who knows? Maybe someday in the near future, a second "season" of *Boys & Toys* might find its way to your Kindle. We may meet a cast of four all-new boys set in the same city with countless new stories to tell, loves to chase, and gasp-worthy trouble to get in. Or perhaps Dean, Garret, Caysen, and Wade have more antics yet to share. Or Sam? Or Jeremy? Or Kevin?

Only time will tell.

And finally, I send my love out to every gay or queer person reading this who, at times, feels like an outsider even among their own kind. You're _not_ alone. Stay true, stay real, and stay good. The world _needs_ your unique, brilliant self to make it that much more special a place to live in. Do you; you're the only one in the world who can.

There is so much beauty, laughter,
and compassion in this world we all share.
Don't let anyone convince you otherwise.

XXOO ~ Daryl

OTHER WORK
BY DARYL BANNER

Male/Male Romance
- Hard For My Boss
- Bromosexual
- Getting Lucky
- Raising Hell
- My Bad Ex-Boyfriend

A "Spruce, Texas" Romance
(sassy, sweet & steamy small-town M/M love stories set in Spruce, Texas)
- Football Sundae
- Born Again Sinner

"Boys & Toys"
(a series of fun & sexy novellas centered around four gay best friends who get into all sorts of trouble in the city)
- Caysen's Catch
- Wade's Workout
- Dean's Dare
- Garret's Game

"The Brazen Boys"
(stand-alone novellas filled of sexual exploration, coming of age, and romantic adventures)
- Dorm Game
- On The Edge
- Owned By The Freshman
- Dog Tags

- Commando (Dog Tags 2)
- All Yours Tonight
- Straight Up
- Houseboy Rules
- Slippery When Wet

A College Obsession Romance
(a new adult romance series)
- Read My Lips
- Beneath The Skin
- With These Hands
- Through Their Eyes: *Five Years Later*

The Beautiful Dead Saga
(a post-apocalyptic fantasy saga)
- The Beautiful Dead
- Dead Of Winter
- Almost Alive
- The Whispers
- The Winters
- The Wakings

The OUTLIER Series
(an epic dystopia saga in six large multi-perspective novels)
- Rebellion
- Legacy
- Reign Of Madness
- Beyond Oblivion
- Weapons Of Atlas
- Gifts Of The Goddess

Kings & Queens *(a companion novella series)*
- The Slum Queen
- The Twice King
- Queen Of Wrath

Printed in the USA
CPSIA information can be obtained
at www.ICGtesting.com
LVHW051930080823
754680LV00004B/262